SO-CFT-749

The

Thirteenth
Earl

ALSO BY EVELYN PRYCE

A Man Above Reproach

The Thirteenth Earl

Evelyn Pryce

Montlake
Romance

This is a work of fiction. Names, characters, organizations, places, events, and incidents are either products of the author's imagination or are used fictitiously.

Text copyright © 2016 Kristin K. Ross
All rights reserved.

No part of this book may be reproduced, or stored in a retrieval system, or transmitted in any form or by any means, electronic, mechanical, photocopying, recording, or otherwise, without express written permission of the publisher.

Published by Montlake Romance, Seattle
www.apub.com

Amazon, the Amazon logo, and Montlake Romance are trademarks of Amazon.com, Inc., or its affiliates.

ISBN-13: 9781503952034
ISBN-10: 1503952037

Cover design by Laura Klynstra

Printed in the United States of America

The Setting

England, 1884. A country estate near Bath. The season is about to change from summer to fall. Some leaves have already drained of color and fallen to the ground, serving as portents to the greenery that still clings to the trees. We are concerned with Spencer House, a lone manor on a hill, where the newlywed Earl and Countess Spencer are throwing a house party.

The Players

- Jonathan Vane, Viscount Thaxton, future thirteenth Earl Vane
- Miss Cassandra Seton, daughter of the Marquess of Dorset
- Dinah Seton, Marchioness of Dorset
- Percival Spencer, Earl Spencer, childhood friend of Thaxton
- Eliza Spencer, Countess Spencer, Percival's wife
- Miles Markwick, Miss Seton's fiancé
- Lucy Macallister, a spiritual medium
- Sutton, a valet

Chapter One

He was going to take out all of his hostility on Percival. Truthfully, Percy was probably the only one who could handle it.

Thaxton raised the sword, fixing the guard against the tip. "Are you sure you want to fence in the library?" he asked, one last time.

"We cannot go outside right now. My relatives are all over the lawn, poking around the estate. We have to hide, of course, but you need to do *something*. En garde," he said.

Percival Spencer—Lord Spencer to those who had not grown up by his side—was possibly the most carefree person Thaxton had ever known.

Jonathan Vane, who had been the Viscount Thaxton since his father required he begin using his courtesy title at university, had never been carefree. Eldest sons were always entitled to use one of their father's honorifics in the case of the highest ranks of the peerage. Thaxton thought the endless procession of names and rules only caused more trouble. His title would eventually be Earl Vane, the thirteenth such luminary. Spencer said it was not so bad, being an earl. Thaxton had been told something different.

"You are a mess," Spencer went on. "London is terrible for you; country air will do you good. Expend the energy you waste moping about your cursed life in some other manner."

Thaxton put the sword at his side, looking down at his wardrobe. His friend probably had a point, but perhaps he just did not care if it looked as if he had stepped off Cork Street. He no longer cared what anyone thought of him.

He had fired his valet months ago and retained only the servants necessary to keep his London rooms reasonably clean. The Vane family's longtime cook made sure the earl and his son ate, but Thaxton thought it best that they kept a minimal amount of staff. People already gossiped enough.

"You are too thin," Spencer continued, relentless in his lecture. "Too thin by half and you have not left your apartments in more than six months. We could carry water from the well by using the bags under your eyes, chap. Do you know that society has begun to call you the Ghost? *The Ghost*, Jonathan. People are talking. Everyone is talking—except you."

Thaxton sighed. He swooshed the sword through the air to hear the sound again. Spencer had fooled him. Drawn him out of the house, trapped him at his country estate for a godforsaken party that would last a fortnight to give him the same speech again. Thaxton had already heard it via letter and his friend's random personal visits. Spencer would not honor his request for solitude.

"You know my father is ill. The Earl Vane is mad, Percy. You have seen him."

"Yes, but that does not mean *your* life is over."

"He is mad," Thaxton averred, tapping the sword against his leg. "He is mad, he cannot take care of himself, and he cannot be among society. I am handling all estate business. He cannot even be trusted to go for a walk. I am the earl in everything but name, and he has three servants dedicated to his whims round the clock."

Spencer shook his head, refusing to get into the conversation again. He raised his blade.

"En garde, Thaxton."

Thaxton looked at Spencer for a moment—his oldest friend, facing him with a thin, dangerous blade. When they were children, before they understood the burden of their titles, they would fence with sticks by the river that ran past the cemetery in the back of Spencer House—the Vanes' country seat a mere fifteen-minute walk away, their families so close they may as well have been one. Dozens of their ancestors lay under the ground that they played on; the two boys pretended to kill each other like knights five feet away from where real ones took eternal rest.

Thaxton stepped one foot back, arranging for the best equilibrium, and lunged forward at Spencer. He blocked in a fluid motion, and a clang rang through the air of the library. Vastly satisfying. A vase shuddered on a pedestal in the corner.

"If your wife finds us in here, she will kill us both," Thaxton said, beginning to enjoy himself. "With our own swords." He crossed his blade with Spencer's and used it to push the earl back. He staggered, clipping his knee on his desk. A stack of papers fluttered to the floor.

"Eliza will understand," he said, straining a bit as he lunged forward again, one bead of sweat trailing down his cheek. "Besides, there is no way she could know—"

"Is that so?" asked the countess from the doorway.

Thaxton used the opportunity, somewhat unfairly, to attack. Spencer parried without even looking at him, smiling at his wife. Eliza inclined her head with fondness, and Thaxton attacked the earl again, on principle. Such happiness as the Spencers displayed always made him more indignant.

Spencer defended again without looking. "Hello, Countess," he said with a grin. "The viscount and I would never be so crass as to duel in the library."

"That vase has been in your family for more than a hundred years, Percival."

Eliza glided into the room, and Thaxton frowned at Spencer's trans-fixed expression. The affliction of love between the new husband and wife permeated any room they were in together. Thaxton knew he was a drunk and a bore, but he had some pride. No woman could ever make him heel the way Eliza had made Spencer.

"Oh, and hello, Miss Seton," Spencer added, leaning to include the form obscured by his wife. "We are unbearably inconsiderate. Miss Seton, the man across from me with the weapon is Jonathan Vane, Viscount Thaxton, horrible rogue and worse swordsman. Thaxton, this is Miss Cassandra Seton, my wife's indispensable friend from Cheltenham, the daughter of the Marquess of Dorset."

Probably as dull as a horseshoe and indoctrinated by that finishing school, Thaxton thought. He could see half of Miss Cassandra Seton's tiny form, almost as if she were hiding in the statuesque Eliza's skirts, which, admittedly, were excessive. Thaxton often thought that women's clothing was designed to thwart men, not attract them.

"Miss Seton is betrothed to Mr. Markwick," Eliza mentioned innocently, "who is finally back in England."

Of course, she would have no idea that this would be the distraction Spencer needed to knock the sword from Thaxton's hand. It went skittering across the room, stopping short of Miss Seton's little tailored boots.

"My sympathies," Thaxton murmured in the direction of Miss Seton, pushing down the bile that rose in his throat at Eliza's words.

This woman was Miles Markwick's fiancée. So, that meant his cousin was home. Thaxton would much rather he had stayed in Scotland. It had been a respite when Miles had run away to the wilds. When Markwick—the most grating man Thaxton had ever come into contact with—was anywhere around him, they could not stop sniping at each other.

Miss Seton stepped out from behind Eliza to pick up the weapon. She wore a day dress of foulard with blue satin trimming, a similar color to the eyes that met his. She handed him back his sword carefully. He had hoped she would be hideous; he had hoped she would be covered in warts. Miles Markwick deserved a wife who would make him miserable to the end of his days.

This woman was none of these things. Her black hair framed the most intriguing face Thaxton had ever seen—neither austere nor cupid, but some sort of in-between.

He took the sword back too quickly, like a child with a toy.

"Viscount Thaxton," she said. "We are soon to be family, as I understand. Do you know your cousin well?"

He could not quite make out her expression. She did not sound friendly. It had been quite some time since Thaxton had spoken to a woman who was neither a relation nor a bed partner. He had no idea how to get a read on her.

"I wager I know him better than you," he said, feeling a bit argumentative, a quality that Miles always brought out in him. "As I understand it, Markwick ran off to Scotland . . . to stall an arranged marriage."

If Spencer had heard him, the conversation would be over. Thaxton knew he was being far too personal—impertinent, even. Fortunately, the earl was listening with a very interested expression to whatever his wife was whispering in his ear.

"Just so," Miss Seton said without so much as a blink of her long eyelashes. "I am that arranged marriage. We were promised when we were both in the cradle. I have met him twice."

Thaxton set the sword down on the table to look away from her keen, assessing gaze for a moment. Her frankness astounded him. It was not a feature of many women of his acquaintance, with the possible exception of Countess Spencer.

He, however, liked it very much.

"How fortunate for you," he said, not sorry for his smirk. She had a face that wanted a flirt, and he was glad to deliver it. "Soon you will know him all too well, and you will find yourself remembering these days with fondness."

"If you use that wit with your tailor, my lord, I see why your clothing does not fit."

He laughed. "I fired him. Why the 'miss,' if I may ask? You are the daughter of a marquess; are you not a lady?"

"Not in the sense they define it. I prefer the 'miss.' I do not like the honorific."

"Little rebel." *Thank goodness for Spencer's continued inattention.* "I do not suppose your parents approve of that."

"They do not pay attention to my wishes." She gave a small smile. "But my friends do. My very best friends call me Cassie."

"Then I shall start with Miss Seton, and endeavor to Cassie."

Miss Seton frowned. Thaxton thought he must be out of practice. He used to throw one of those smirks from twenty paces without a doubt that it would land well. This one did not.

"Good day, Lord Thaxton," she said, turning abruptly to rejoin Eliza.

He smiled at her back. If he was to be stranded in Bath, Miss Seton was, too.

∞

Cassandra excused herself from Spencer's library, ignoring Eliza's worried look. She needed a moment alone, and the gardens beckoned. Eliza had planted them specifically to attract butterflies; the air felt soft as she entered the green shadowy paths.

Miles would be there tomorrow, after she had not set eyes on him in nine years. The last time she had seen him, he had clasped her hand and promised he would return. That he needed to seek his fortune and assess his decrepit Scottish estate, abandoned by his father when the upkeep had gotten to be too much. He would come back for her, he had reassured.

Tomorrow would be a promise fulfilled, nine torturous years later.

Cassandra sat down on a bench in a little copse. She knew she should be happy. She had instead rocketed through every emotion but happiness since learning the news of his return, anger being the primary offender. Nine years alone since her age of majority, nine years trapped in limbo, obligated to marry this man she did not even know.

She had to turn down Lord Beaumont when he swore his devotion, even though he would have made a fine husband. Thomas Amberson, a baronet, would have been able to provide enough for a sensible life, but Cassandra had told him no as well. She had no choice. Her father had promised away both her and her dowry in a businesslike deal at her age of majority.

"Excuse me, Miss Seton."

And on top of it all, Lord Thaxton. The viscount had followed her. Perhaps it was the setting, but his dark-brown hair reminded her of a garden, this one gone to seed—tendrils curling at his neck, untamed. Thaxton's cravat had been tied by careless hands and not by any self-respecting valet.

The combination should not have been attractive.

"Forgive me," he continued. "I should not have been so flip about Miles. As you know, he is my cousin, but we have not had an easy history."

"Apology accepted," she said. She hoped he would leave it at that. Instead, he sat down beside her, in a cloud of whisky and some scent beneath—what? Something exotic, new to her nostrils.

"I can tell you about him," he said, folding his hands as if he was a proper gentleman, which he was visibly not. "You must be curious."

"About Miles? I will soon find out all about him, I am sure. He arrives on the morrow and will stay with us the length of the house party. The Spencers have been very accommodating."

"Percy is too permissive. I would never have Markwick at my house." Thaxton tilted his head toward her, and she could not avoid a panoramic view of his sharp jaw, covered as it was with beard growth. Cassandra blessed the beard, because she did not want to be exposed to the naked power of that face.

"You apologize," she said, instead of anything that she had been thinking, "then continue to be rude."

"Merely honest." He smiled, a strange, lenient thing that eased the tiny lines of worry nestled around his eyes. "I do not mean to offend you, but I find it interesting that you know nothing of the man who will be your husband."

"You do not like him."

"Oh, everybody likes Miles Markwick. You mustn't listen to me; I am the exception to the rule. Miles is the one who stole my whirligigs. Miles is the one who tattled on me to my governess. He is the one who replaced my brandy with rainwater at Oxford. He never liked me and thus never gave me the opportunity to like him."

"We should not be alone here," she said.

"I know. I find it exciting. And you?"

Cassandra scooted back on the bench. The truth was, she definitely felt the same, but voicing it would not do. "Surely I do not."

"Pity. I was thinking I might like to kiss you."

A few things about the sentence stunned her—its bluntness, the unceremonious tone, the fact that it did not sound like a lie. To what end would he say such a thing? If it were just to shock her, she would not give him the satisfaction.

"You cannot do that. And you well know it."

"Hmm," he said, pulling back a bit and shaking his head. "You are right. Too much chance of discovery. You would not want to be saddled to me. Miles is a nitwit, but I am unacceptable."

Cassandra ignored the part of her that felt disappointed. She had not been kissed since Amberson had been so bold at the Solstice Ball. That made for a total of three kisses in all those years, including one from Miles himself. It seemed a shame that she should not experience even just one more. And, she admitted to herself, she very much wanted to kiss Lord Thaxton.

Even if he did smell like a distillery.

"You are too, too presumptuous," she said, grasping hold of her composure. "I am looking forward to getting to know Miles, and I have no fear about my nuptials."

Cassandra felt she could taste that lie. Something passed over the viscount's face, a shutter going up. He stood, bowing his head to her.

"I should go before I say anything else to make you dislike me," he said. "Good day, Miss Seton."

"Good day," she said to his back, his departure leaving her slightly stunned, as if his presence had been a poisoned dart.

❧

Her daze continued as she helped Eliza plan the dinner party and unpacked her trunks. Two weeks. Two weeks adrift in the countryside with her future husband and all she could think about was his haunted-looking cousin.

Cassandra observed the drawing room where the guests of the Spencers' house party were gathering before dinner. Eliza's family, decidedly less distinguished than Percy's, could be identified by their cooing enthusiasm. The earl's family, unlike the young earl himself, was a mostly staid and static affair, much concerned with image.

She played a game of titles, as she was wont to do when passing time. It always amused her how organized the social hierarchy was, how ingrained they all were to respect it. The highest level of peerage in this room was a duke, which she knew because she had overhead a conversation. So, one presumed duke in attendance but not one she had been introduced to. She discreetly folded one finger back to keep count. Two earls, Spencer included. She folded back two more fingers and squinted her eyes to peer across the room. A smattering of random lords and one lonely knight of the crown.

Precisely one viscount.

Cassandra lost track of her tally. She didn't want to be looking at the despicable viscount, but there was nothing else to do. Eliza had gone to check on the dining area. A local chaplain went on about that week's sermon, and she certainly couldn't listen to that. The only thing left to do was to look at Thaxton, who was leaning against a bookshelf on the far end of the room. Must he lean on everything?

He was alone, of course, glaring at the assembled crowd. He looked a little neater than earlier; he had made an effort to clean up for dinner. His wispy brown hair benefited from a brush, and his eyes—a bluish gray that sometimes looked green—were a touch sharper. Not that a bit of tidying and brushing could cover the permanent scowl lines.

"It is terribly rude to be gawking in a social situation."

Cassandra's head snapped to her stepmother's voice, low at her ear and containing its familiar hint of displeasure. The Marchioness of Dorset's short stature was no impediment to her bearing, however, because she still managed to be terrifying. She kept her hair hidden under an elaborate wig that had a tinge of pink, something that she'd decided looked fashionably French. When Cassandra's mother died five years before, Dinah had sniffed around the marquess until he noticed her. It had not taken long—Cassandra's father viewed marriage as a transaction, and Dinah was from an old family, the widow of an earl to boot. Cassandra suspected that Dinah had been around for a long time before her mother had even fallen ill; she had once heard her grandmother say the marquess "did not care for fidelity." As soon as the proper mourning period was over, Dinah became the new Lady Dorset, which all but confirmed her suspicions. Since then, the woman had been desperate to get Cassandra out of the house.

"I apologize," Cassandra said. "I am merely anxious about Miles's arrival."

"I am sure he will be just as charming as he was."

"I quite agree." *Even if the most exciting thing about it is getting away from your meddling,* she thought but did not say.

"We shall begin planning the wedding straightaway," Lady Dorset said, for the fifth time in two days. "Tonight you will be escorted by Malcolm Hewett—Baron Islay—you remember him from last season. The rest of our time here you will be with Miles, of course. I believe you should wear the lavender tulle tomorrow."

This was usually the point where Cassandra started ignoring her stepmother's rambling. All that was required of her were smiles and nods. Eventually, a patroness pulled Lady Dorset's attention away. Cassandra's eyes started to wander, inevitably to the viscount.

What a horrible man. He seemed bent on insulting her from the moment they met. Cassandra had not felt at ease since the encounter with him, though Eliza had apologized profusely. She'd said that Thaxton was prone to offend anyone who stepped into his rarefied air. She frowned. The viscount tilted his head to the ceiling, presumably to glower at a sconce. He seemed a very angry man—but in a muted sense. Not the type to get violent, the type to simmer quietly. For a titled man with presumably few worries, he had the air of someone who had been denied something. It was not anger on his face, she decided. It was frustration. He was quite attractive, she had to admit, but it hid beneath layers of insomnia and poor manners.

Someone touched her on the arm, and Cassandra turned to find Eliza, a look of suspicion on her face.

"You are staring, Cassie," she said.

"At what? No."

"I should have known," Eliza said. "When I first met that man, I thought of you. Handsome, brooding, witty—he is your every weakness. He is entirely unsuitable for a proper lady, or I would have introduced you earlier. Also, you are engaged."

"I am, which is why I was not staring at Lord Thaxton."

"But should you find yourself looking his way, you would do well to stop. Even if Miles weren't arriving tomorrow, Thaxton's reputation is among the worst. He is practically a leper. He is Percy's oldest friend, but do you see him talking to anyone?"

"Not that I have been keeping a vigil, but no. Ah, wait. He talked to the dowager earlier."

Eliza raised her regal eyebrows to tell Cassandra that she was onto her. "Tell me you haven't been counting how many glasses of brandy he has drunk."

"Too many," Cassandra muttered.

"Best to leave it alone," Eliza pronounced, steering Cassandra to her spot in the dinner procession line, away from any view of Thaxton.

And leave it alone she did. Cassandra only looked his way once or twice or fifteen times during the whole meal.

❦

He was not going to look at her. Thaxton mustered every bit of self-discipline he had. He resisted, though he could feel Miss Seton's eyes making a feast of him. He did not look at her. Would not. Could not.

He did not look at her in the parlor; he did not look at her during dinner. He endeavored to lower his standards to join in the dull-headed conversation at the table, which turned out mildly successful. He managed to keep down his food, or to push it around his plate enough that it appeared he was eating. All the while, he did not look at her.

The first time he felt any sort of a spark when he looked in a woman's eyes and it was Miles Markwick's bloody fiancée. The irony of it might have been delicious, if he could taste anything at all anymore.

He retired to the parlor with the men after dinner, per Spencer's request. Thaxton did not much care for talk of horseflesh or politics, and feigning interest became difficult. He left for his room as soon as he could; he found he would much rather obliterate his brain with alcohol while alone.

Back in his chambers, he tried to read himself to sleep, a trick that sometimes worked if he found a particularly dry book. It did not work this evening. He blew out his candles thrice, only to light them again, as his wakeful mood persisted. Unbidden, he wondered what Miss Seton was doing. Probably sleeping, dreaming of damned Miles, who did not deserve his good fortune. He had another glass of brandy and prayed for sleep.

Yet another unanswered prayer.

As he turned another boring page, he could swear he heard moaning. Not groans of pleasure, but thin and disembodied wails. Thaxton was used to the noises of a house settling, as he had studied them many sleepless nights at his own home. The sounds echoing in the hall of Spencer House did not match, nor did they seem real. Neither prospect was appetizing. True wails would have macabre implications. But if they were not real, then he was mad.

Likely the latter, he thought. He set his glass down and put his ear to the door, feeling silly about it. For a moment there was silence, then another noise—keen, plaintive, and protracted.

"Good god," he said aloud, though he was alone.

What if someone was in trouble? He was only half-dressed, having abandoned both jacket and gloves, shirt untucked and waistcoat unbuttoned, white tie hanging loose on one side underneath his collar. Thaxton tapped his foot, staring at the back of the door. He crossed his arms and rocked back and forth on his heels. It seemed as if he could not in good conscience ignore what he was hearing. Unless he wasn't hearing anything. In that case, he might be discovered by a footman and look like a buffoon, earning his nickname by wandering witlessly around the estate, chasing after voices that no one else heard.

Well past shame, he turned the doorknob and peeked into the hallway. Nothing. He was about to shut the door and drink to the bottom of the bottle in humiliation when the sound came again. This time it was clearer, winding its way from downstairs. He could not believe it had not woken everyone else on the floor, but he was the only one in the hallway. For a few seconds, he could not force his feet to move.

When he finally did, the creaks of the floorboards rasped under his boots. He could hear someone snoring, probably Lord Hartwell, who slumbered three doors down. Thaxton crept down the stairs, wishing he had thought to bring a candle. Everyone was abed, leaving the house almost black. He stopped at the bottom of the stairs, hearing the sound again. Improbably, it had grown quieter and sounded farther away. His best guess at its source was the so-called blue parlor at the far end of the ground floor, a lush cavern that had been a favorite of Spencer's mother before she relocated to the dowager house on the edge of the estate.

The hallway carpet muted the sound of his boots, not that anyone would have heard him. The ground floor was deserted, not even a footman in sight. Thaxton realized he had no idea what time it was—lately, time had become an imprecise thing, slipping by or crawling, passing unmarked.

He froze with his hand on the doorknob, remembering that the wood creaked when you opened it. The dowager countess hated interruption, and that very creak had preceded lectures when Spencer and Thaxton were children. Going to the blue parlor, hearing that creak: it always meant they were in trouble.

This time, after the creak, he saw Miss Seton.

She yelped, and her hands flew to her mouth to stifle the sound. Her skin practically glowed in the moonlight, and by god, Thaxton was annoyed. How dare she look like that, and how dare she be there now. Without stopping to think, he shut the door behind him. Her eyes widened, a persistent type of blue.

"What," he demanded, "are you doing here?"

"Shh," she said, doing a frantic dance with her hands. He frowned. A woman who gestured excessively—not a good sign.

Thaxton advanced on her, a bit too hostile, judging from the way she shrank back. "Are you wailing in this room like a wraith?"

"Lower your voice, my lord," she whispered with a slight sarcastic emphasis on "lord" that aggravated him further. "No, I was not. But I gather you heard it as well."

"I have not heard it since being in the same room with you."

After having reprimanded him for volume, she laughed loudly.

"You cannot be serious. You think I was making that noise?"

"Clearly," he said, studying her. He moved closer on instinct, more effortlessly than he had before. "Now I am just wondering why."

She scrunched her nose. "You are drunk."

"More often than not." He shrugged.

"I did not make that noise, Lord Thaxton. I came down here to search for it. I am sober, unlike you, and I know I heard a woman howling. Not a woman." She paused for effect. "A ghost."

He could not help but cringe at the word, hoping the darkness masked his expression. It was a constant reminder of what society thought he was: a walking dead man haunting their streets. The whispers about his family had been going on for years. Surely Miss Seton had heard them already, or the countess had told her. Jonathan Vane and his father, the mad earl, hiding in plain sight. The ton had a hundred theories regarding their fate and situation.

"You believe in ghosts?" he asked.

"I do not know," Miss Seton said. "I suppose I do not discount them."

She certainly looked enough like an apparition. The blue of the room's furnishings bounced off the color in her eyes, making them flash like ice. Her hair fell in loose, glossy curls meandering down her back. Thaxton had failed to realize she was in a nightgown. Now that he had, a stab of desire entered him, uninvited.

It cut straight through his haze. As opposed to the structured dress she'd worn during the day, the gauzy confection she wore now suggested her curves, falling over them. All it would take would be one good grip on the hem and he could . . .

"Lord Thaxton." Miss Seton had her hand on her hip. He refocused his eyes to find her blushing most charmingly. "I asked if you had ever heard anything like that before. The noise."

Damn. He shook himself internally. He should have thought to bed a woman before leaving London—his urges were going to run wild in a secluded estate filled with women. Or, were he to be honest, this particular woman.

"Not a noise like that," he said. "I spent the majority of my childhood in this house, and I have heard many unexplained noises here—but never that. It sounded like crying. Mourning. Did it not?"

"Exactly that. I was worried that someone was in danger."

"Yet the house is still."

"Quite."

For some reason, that particular alchemy of words stole the rest from the both of them. Thaxton noted that hunger touched the edges of her cool gaze, even as he felt it heat the air around him. She closed the distance between them hazily, as if she were half-asleep.

"We were imagining things," he said, finding that he was peering down on her vexing face, far too close. She had very long eyelashes, a fringe he wanted to touch with his lips. He took a shallow breath, because a deeper one would cause their bodies to collide. "We should go to bed."

Her eyes widened. He had not meant to say it like an invitation, but it had come out that way.

"Separately," he clarified.

She did not respond, for some reason. He shifted, wondering if he should look away. For an illogical moment, he thought she was waiting for him to kiss her. But that could not be; it was not within the realm of possibility for him.

"Miss Seton?" he whispered.

She tilted her head to the side and smiled. Though it was dim, he could see her looking at his lips. He was not imagining things.

"Oh, hell."

The brandy pumping through his veins made the foolhardy act of pulling her into his arms easy. But next she would slap him and it would be over—surely that would be the outcome.

"I will admit, I know what you are thinking," he said, idly running a hand down her cheek to test her reaction. "Kissing you is a terrible idea. A wonderful and terrible idea. My favorite kind."

Was she ever going to talk? He ran a thumb over her bottom lip, trying to tease out a response. If she kept gazing as she was, all dreamy-eyed and hot, he would have no choice but to—

Thaxton was absolved of completing the thought when she took his face in her hands and did what he had been waffling about.

Chapter Two

Cassandra could not wait any longer. The more he talked, the more he made excuses for something they both wanted. She pulled his face down to hers, her fingers running through his scratchy beard. After all, it was just a kiss, she reasoned.

Except when they entwined.

Thaxton's arms curled around her back, the heavy wool of his coat scraping the flimsy fabric of her nightgown. As much as he had been talking, he had also been thinking about an embrace, judging from the way he clutched her. He did indeed taste like brandy, but what was bitter in the glass was sweet on his soft lips.

Mistake, she thought frantically. *This is a mistake.* It felt nothing like a lark, nothing like a last flight of fancy before she started her life as Mrs. Miles Markwick. She wanted to take it back, but his hand was on her head, fingers weaved in her hair, holding her fast. The only sound in the entire universe was his exhale.

"Miss Seton," he said, his mouth now behind her earlobe, his hair tickling her cheek, "you are so lovely. I wish it were not so."

She could not think of a reply, not through the shivers overtaking her.

Thaxton resumed kissing her without further comment. She tried to match him but found that the force of it had stolen her senses. None among Amberson, Miles, or the random footman had been so assertive in his amours. During those encounters, she mostly wondered if she was doing it wrong, fumbling.

Not with Thaxton—she could not think at all. She was all too aware of her body as he guided the embrace by winding a hand through the back of her hair. Just then, she felt his tongue teasing the crease of her lips. She pushed back on his chest, resistant to the new feeling, but not committed enough to shove.

He released her, standing back. He looked more unkempt than before, as if that were possible, and Cassandra realized that she had been ravaging him equal to his mauling of her.

"Most peculiar," he said into the silence.

"Forgive me," she said, unsure where the apology came from.

"Never." He smiled. "I will never forgive you."

"Then you must forget."

"Again, no." He looked down, the remains of that smile on his face, even as they both returned to their senses. "But I do understand. Go to sleep, my dear Miss Seton. When you awake tomorrow, your prince will have arrived."

It took Cassandra a moment to realize he was talking about Miles. Took her a moment to remember that Miles was a person who existed. Guilt bloomed in the pit of her stomach.

"Our secret," he said, reading her face. "It meant nothing."

She nodded. "Nothing." Nothing, except she was still vibrating a little. "There is no more wailing . . ."

"Perhaps the ghost does not like kissing."

She gave a nervous laugh, and he leaned forward to squeeze her hand.

"I know I cannot see you to your room, but I will be behind you, be assured. Once you are safely returned, the moment you close your door, this will have never happened. Consider it a dream, complete with unexplained phenomena."

"Thank you," she said with gratitude.

"Go," he said. "Go."

Cassandra laid a final kiss against his cheek, but she felt him shrink away too soon. He was very good at cutting off, a skill she envied. She kept jumping at every noise on the walk back to her room, not so much due to fear of ghosts but to a creeping guilt at sneaking around at night and getting kissed by strangers. The estate was dead quiet, one torch burning low in the entrance hall. Though she could not hear or see Lord Thaxton, she felt him there, twenty steps or more behind, a trailing impression.

She stopped in front of her chamber door, his words ringing in her ears. She didn't want to think it was a dream. She didn't want to forget it. She wanted to know more. She turned around to see Thaxton lurking at the corner, his legs crossed as leaned again against the wall, waiting for her to be safely in her room. He raised a finger to shush her and then nodded to the door, telling her to go in.

She touched a hand to her lips and then turned it toward him. His mouth quirked up, and he mimed catching the kiss she had thrown. Then he gave three little flicks of his hand, a "move along" gesture. She returned them with one last smile before turning away.

By the time Cassandra closed the door, she knew she was not in love with Miles.

She slept poorly, with questions running through her mind. Though she did wake a few times and listen before falling back asleep, she heard no more wailing. Perhaps Thaxton was right and the ghost did not like scandalous behavior. Cassandra's cheeks burned when she thought of it. Before she knew it, dawn streamed in through the windows. She was just opening her eyes when Lady Dorset breezed in, fully dressed and wide-awake. Today her hair formed a bluish confection, wobbling slightly with her every word.

"He's here!" she said, upbeat. "The servants are bringing Miles's luggage in at this very moment. He immediately asked how you fare. What a good sign!"

Cassandra rubbed her eyes. The first man on her mind when she awoke had been the viscount. There was no way she was letting Lady Dorset know that.

"Now remember, Cassandra. You have been groomed for this all of your life. Being a wife is the greatest adventure a woman can have."

Cassandra pulled herself up in bed.

"I had rather hoped it would be more like finding a fellow adventurer."

Lady Dorset was rooting through the bottles on Cassandra's vanity. She picked up the perfume, smelled it, and wrinkled her nose.

"I do not know what you mean by that, nor do I wish to." She glanced over at the bed with censure. "Get up, Cassandra. We haven't time to dally."

The marchioness threw a robe at her.

"Your friend the countess has been so kind as to arrange a private breakfast for you and Mr. Markwick, which is a great opportunity to entrance his eye. You have been apart a great while; you must look your best. You have already slept late."

It was true. Cassandra had sent her lady's maid away twice. She was tired—her heart hammered into the silent room for at least an hour after Thaxton kissed her. It was difficult to sleep like that.

She smiled through her teeth at Lady Dorset. "Would you mind vacating so that I may dress?"

"Twenty minutes," she snapped. "Do not keep Miles waiting."

Almost as soon as Lady Dorset left, Eliza came in. Cassandra sagged a bit in relief at the thought of her friend's honesty. She had likely been up for hours already, in a cashmere day costume with a pointed bodice, feathers from a bird of paradise placed artfully in her bun.

"Have you seen Miles yet? Is he handsome?" Cassandra asked. It was a shame that she had no idea.

"You will think he is. He has a face like a fox."

"Is he happy?"

Eliza sat down on the edge of the bed, nudging aside one of the canopy curtains. "Are you?"

Cassandra's maid entered, arranging her toiletries with a more frantic hand than usual. She supposed she should feel like a proper bride, brimming with excitement.

"I am . . . not unhappy."

Eliza perched on the edge of the bed.

"I understand that this is challenging. How long ago had he written?"

"Last week . . . the abrupt announcement that he was returning. But before that, it had been three months. At first, his letters were so romantic. Describing the countryside and how we might travel it together, how he longed for me, visions of our future together. Positively lyrical. And yet in the past two years, he seemed to send the same letter— *Thank you for waiting for me. I promise I am securing our future. I miss you so.'* Perfunctory, like I had turned into an obligation. Does that sound like the behavior of a man who truly missed me?"

"Give him a chance to woo you again, dear," Eliza said, patting her hand. "I have a light breakfast for you and Miles, while the rest of the party is entertained in the garden. I thought it best that we have the morning alone without the interference of Lady Dorset."

"I have always thought you were brilliant." Cassandra smiled, stretching into the robe with a yawn. "I am so tired, Eliza. Your house is haunted."

"The groans? It is an old estate, and the winds are high in these hills. You will be used to it within a few days."

"No, dear. It is definitely a ghost."

And the Ghost, himself, but Eliza needn't know about that.

"Oh, Cassie. Come now. There are no such things. I admit, the house makes noises at night, but it is not spirits. Just a normal house, creaking as it sleeps."

"That is not what it sounds like. It sounds like a woman, crying, grieving. It is awful, and I cannot believe you did not hear it."

Cassandra sat straight, stretching her back, as the lady's maid started brushing her hair. She studied herself in the mirror, wondering if she was as attractive as she had been the last time Miles had seen her. Older, to be sure, but not much changed. If he thought her beautiful before, he still would. She hoped.

"Well then, my dove," Eliza said, standing and smoothing her skirts, "I shall see you downstairs in twenty minutes. Your beau awaits."

"Yes," she replied vaguely. "Thank you, Eliza."

All too soon, she was descending the stairs. At the bottom, Miles stood with his arms behind his back. His neck craned as he saw her slippers. His black hair swooped across his forehead, almost covering one of his dark-brown eyes. At the moment, they radiated warmth. It calmed Cassandra's heart a bit when their gazes met—he looked sincerely happy to see her. His smile sent hopefulness in her direction. But what had he been doing in Scotland? All that time?

As she got closer, she felt a wave of anger propel her forward. He had left her adrift for nine years, while people talked behind her back. As if he had no idea how vicious society could be. She often felt alone at all the balls she was invited to, knowing that as soon as she left a conversation, there was a person whispering about poor Miss Seton and how embarrassing it must be to be abandoned by your betrothed.

He held out both of his hands as she reached him, and she put hers in them because it was what was expected. She watched his eyes as he bent over to kiss her fingers. He had done this on the balcony at her debutante ball, whispering that she was the loveliest woman he had ever seen. He had the same look in his eyes now, and it sent a bolt of hope through her—the thought that they could not only repair things but also be happy.

"Cassandra," he said. "I have imagined this very moment for so long."

"Hello, Mr. Markwick," she said, hoping she affected a light tone. Cassandra had played this moment over in her mind a hundred times. Sometimes she welcomed him with open arms, grateful to finally see him; sometimes she slapped him. She wanted to do both now that the time had come.

"I do think you should call me Miles. You used to."

"Yes. Miles."

"Are you not happy to see me?" he asked, looking perplexed.

"Of course I am," she said with what she hoped was a serviceable smile. But behind Miles, she could see through into the breakfast parlor, where Thaxton was serenely biting into toast. He was not supposed to be there.

Eliza had said it was private. The viscount had shaved, was neat as a pin, and she was lost. She wrenched her eyes back to Miles, who now regarded her with wariness.

"You do not seem it," he said. "And I cannot blame you. I am the worst man in the world for leaving such a beautiful flower behind."

Cassandra knew that this proclamation should have made her heart thump, or whatever happened when one's paramour paid a compliment. It should have given her hope. In the parlor, Thaxton had moved on to a plate of sausage.

She put her arm through Miles's. "Shall we go to breakfast?"

⚯

He could not believe his good fortune, until he saw Miss Seton coming down the stairs into the arms of Miles Markwick. Thaxton felt sorry for a fleeting moment, before he let a grin break on his face. Inadvertently plundering their reunion meal provided him with more than just a nice repast. Miss Seton had seen him, and the look on her face gave a pretty reward. Though he knew he would never have her, he had awoken with a mighty urge to impress the woman.

Miles swung the parlor door all the way open, as he always did with doors, making it crash against the wall with a careless bounce. The oaf.

"Thaxton," he said, startled. "What the blazes are you doing here?"

He stood, dropping a small bow of his head, directed at Cassandra, not Miles.

"Eating. The morning's food in the other room was gone. The countess has thoughtfully provided a second set, it seems." He popped another piece of the toast in his mouth and raised his eyebrows playfully. "Good morning, Miss Seton."

"Good morning, Lord Thaxton."

She was flushed. The pleasure filling his veins was worth all the poking and prodding from Spencer's uncompromising valet. And even better, Miles's expression had turned over into ugly, barely concealed anger.

"I see you have met my cousin," he said tightly. "I assure you he is not a good representation of the rest of my family."

"Welcome home, Miles," Thaxton said, as he sank into the seat that was meant for Markwick. He helped himself to the eggs and sausage, finding that sobriety and satisfaction boosted his appetite. "Do keep your temper. There is a lady present."

The lady in question, no meek miss, took the seat at the head of the table. Miles scurried to pull her chair out, but his manners were a half step off. In order to seat himself, he had to borrow a chair from the corner, far too plush to properly fit at the table. He sank in, creating the illusion that he was a child, his feet scraping at the floor and his chin near the plates. This might be Thaxton's best morning in years.

"Allow me to explain, Cassandra," Miles said, turning his back on Thaxton. "Despite anything my cousin may have told you, I bear him no ill will. I pity him. His sickness has made him paranoid."

"I am not sick," he snapped, unable to catch the protest. "My father is."

"Ah, yes," Miles said, swiveling. "How is the Earl Vane?"

"His situation does not change."

"How awful," Miss Seton said, meeting his gaze from behind Miles's glare. "It must be difficult for you."

Thaxton felt a weird stab in the area of his heart. He did not like it.

"It is . . . manageable," he said, cursing the slight hitch in his voice.

A silence spread in which Miles faded out of the room and Thaxton could only see Miss Seton, her dark eyebrows a straight slash of disquiet across her forehead.

"If you would excuse us," Miles said, "as much as I sympathize with your plight, Thaxton, my fiancée and I have a lot to catch up on."

"That is not my fault," he returned with a serenity he had not felt for months. "It is yours."

"Let it go, Miles, please," Cassandra said, with a bit of a waver. "Lord Thaxton obviously needs to eat . . ."

"Obviously," Thaxton agreed.

". . . and he is doing us no harm. Ignore him and tell me about Scotland."

Miles made a solid go of sitting upright in his chair. Thaxton snickered.

"There is not much to tell," Miles said, speaking directly to Cassandra. "I was hoping to find an occupation in order to supplement your dowry, along with returning my family's abandoned Scottish estate to its former glory. I knew that once my father passed, I would have to deal with expenses on my own. But, I tell you, after growing up around such excess—the viscount here would be a good example—it is quite hard to do an honest day's work."

"Pssh," Thaxton said, wiping his mouth. He had decimated a good portion of their food. "Growing up around nobles is not the reason you have trouble being a man."

Though she might have denied it, he saw Miss Seton smile. Miles was apparently deciding whether or not to retort. He chose to continue.

"As it stands, I found nothing that would suit me, except possibly academic work. The estate renovations have progressed enough to make it our home and will conclude once we have . . . a bit more money to spend. But, my darling, how have things been here?"

Thaxton tried to clamp his mouth shut, to not say anything. It was futile. He could not let the man's utter neglect and insensitivity stand.

"Miles, have you any idea," he cut in, "what Miss Seton must have had to endure the years you left her here? What you sentenced her to, playing around in Scotland? If you think gossip is anything less than vicious, you are naive."

Miss Seton's mouth fell open a bit, a delicate oval. Conversation at the table ground to an unceremonious halt, saved only by the entry of Spencer and Eliza.

"Miles," Spencer said, not exactly with warmth. "I trust you had a safe trip."

"Too long. I was *so* anxious to get back," Miles answered, dewy-eyed.

Don't scoff, Jonathan, Thaxton told himself. *Just don't.* He noticed the countess fix on him, regarding his presence as an intrusion.

"What a nice surprise, Lord Thaxton," she said, with forced sincerity. Eliza hated when things did not go according to her plans, and Thaxton at the private breakfast had not been in her plan, he knew. "We expected just Miles and Cassandra." She took in his appearance. "You look well."

"I feel magnificent," he said, which was the truth.

Spencer laughed. "Wonders never cease. Say, Thaxton, we were about to invite Miles and Cassandra to tour the gardens. You are welcome to join us."

Thaxton saw Eliza flick her eyes at her husband in reprimand.

"Thank you, Spencer," he said. "I think I will."

He rose, pushing his empty plate away.

"Finish your food, Cassie," Eliza said, seeing that Cassandra had been about to stand. Thaxton's weird ebullience verged on disconcerting. He gave her a lazy smile as the countess continued. "Relax, talk with Mr. Markwick, and meet us in the garden when you're through."

"Thank you, Countess," Miles said, as if he had been holding a breath in for a very long time.

Thaxton followed the Spencers as they left, but he could not resist clapping Miles on the back on the way out. Miles glared at him, and he returned the dazzling smile he normally reserved for placating children.

Spencer grabbed Thaxton's arm and held him back as Eliza went ahead, floating as she always did. They strolled down the hallway to the outside while they talked.

"I have seen that look before. You kissed that girl," he said. "Might be a bad move, mate."

"To be fair—she kissed me."

"However it happened. I am sure you put up a fight."

Thaxton could have argued that point. He felt he had presented Miss Seton with some very good reasons as to why they should not embrace. For Spencer's sake, he did not press it. He just said, "It was inevitable."

"Even so. The only outcome of this is trouble. You will ruin the house party with scandal, and Eliza will have my head on a stick."

The countess looked back. "What are you two whispering about?"

"I never whisper"—Spencer smiled at her—"outside of the bedroom."

He lifted the heavy latch on the gate to the gardens—a giant arching monstrosity, old as the ground it was hammered into and elaborately structured with lengths of metal vine. The sunlight shone through it, casting the pattern in shadow on the grass.

All the way back to the first countess, Spencer House's gardens had been improved and expanded by the lady of the house but never changed in any significant way. This gave the vast area a kind of stylized disorder, an equation with unequal parts. Eliza had added the newest piece—the butterfly clearing comprising flowers that were known to attract the winged insects—which she had yet to properly name. Not all of her predecessors had been so discerning. The third countess had built a copse of sculptures but had been unable to stop buying them, so that area became overrun with cherubs and angels and goddesses. The seventh countess did not have a knack for devising landscapes, so the Marion Quarter, as her contribution was called, exploded with clashing colors and contrasting plants. The fifth countess devised the giant hedge labyrinth.

Thaxton stopped in the main clearing. He could hear an orchestra warming up for a luncheon concert, Miss Seton would be joining them, and there had been no frenzied letters from his father. Air brushed his face lightly, a novelty since shaving the beard.

It felt like a good day.

After an hour at breakfast, Cassandra thought that Miles Markwick was handsome, well spoken, and amiable, but she did not want to marry him. He kept talking, doggedly saying nothing of import. It was almost as if he was afraid that letting her talk would be dangerous. She would have the chance to bring up their long estrangement.

"We should join the others in the garden, don't you think, my dear?" Markwick's smile thinned his lips. She could not help comparing it with Thaxton's wide mouth, the prominent bow at the top and that plump bottom lip. She forced her awareness back to the present moment, where Miles was still talking, feeling no small amount of shame about her wandering thoughts.

"Before we do, I feel I should warn you. Though the viscount seems as if he is a charming eccentric, he is a nasty chap. We should do our best to stay away from him."

She was interested in this. "Did he wrong you in some way?"

"I suppose not," Miles mused. "We never got on. Boys, playing childhood pranks. His father always seemed to like me better and once even said he wished Thaxton could be more like me. Thaxton is in the branch of our family that thinks itself loftier; they would never visit our extended cousins, nor lower themselves to stay on outside of fashionable areas or posh country houses, like Spencer House. I think the viscount looked down on me in some ways because I would never be titled. He is like that. Superficial."

Cassandra pursed her lips. That could be true, but it could be false. She had known Thaxton for a day. But she did not find him to be posturing; he was far too self-aware for that. She also thought he hated himself.

"My dear. What are you thinking?"

"I was thinking we should join the others," she lied. "You need not worry about Thaxton. It is a big house party; we can avoid him."

"That is exactly what I wanted to hear," he said, kissing her fingertips. His eyes had taken on a seductive air, like they had the one magical night that they kissed. He had been wearing white, like any respectable fairy-tale prince, his dark hair a dashing sweep atop his head, slick and neat.

Miles offered his arm, smiling at her in a way that seemed too suggestive. She knew she should feel some sort of stirring, but it did not come. As they walked down the hallway, she went through her options. She could appeal to her father, tell him she did not want to marry. There was little chance of success that way. She could run away. This, too, seemed like it would be a disaster. Cassandra knew she was clever, but she also knew she would not last a week without a sure place to sleep.

". . . and so, I became fascinated with it," Miles said, finishing a sentence that she had not heard the beginning of.

"Pardon?"

"Spiritualism, Cassandra," he said, sounding a bit exasperated. "You seem to get distracted easily. I know that are you used to discussing what you will wear to the next ball, but this is a bit more philosophical. I was telling you that while in Scotland, I met a group of people who can communicate with the spirit world. It is most mesmerizing."

"Oh! I have heard stories about that," she exclaimed, unable to mask her excitement. Communicating with spirits? It was just what she needed to solve the nettling issue of the wailing woman. "We—I heard noises in the estate last night. This whole house seems . . . eerie.

Could we investigate it? Do you think there are people in England who do the same?"

Miles squeezed through the half-open gate, tugging her along with him. A nearby vine caught on her skirt and fell in a green coil to the ground. Cassandra loved the gardens at Spencer House, for all their eccentricity. She loved them precisely for that reason.

He smiled at her in the afternoon sun.

"Do you remember when we signed the marriage contract? It was only the second day we laid eyes on each other."

"Of course I do; I was barely eighteen. That contract has shaped my life."

Miles smiled at what he thought was an endorsement of the contract and took her hand, tucking it into his elbow.

"You were so nervous. You had no reason to be; I thought you beautiful and perfect. But somehow the nervousness made you even more delightful."

"What a strange way to meet," she mused. "Introduced by our parents, but already promised. I was told I would marry you before I had ever seen you." She dropped her voice an octave. "The Marquess of Dorset gives this young woman in exchange for these working coalfields. Please sign here."

"I was lucky to sign," he said. "A few coalfields are nothing compared with you. My family got the better deal."

She smiled at his pretty words. Words she had not seen in letters for some years. She also knew it was a lie. The coalfields Miles's family had given up for a connection to a marquess's family had been worth a fortune, easily enough that Miles would not have had to worry about money for the rest of his life. His father could not have known that, but hindsight made no difference. The senior Mr. Markwick passed away months ago, having never remarried after Miles's mother died in a carriage accident when he was seven and in the little school he attended in his youth. When speaking of it, he always stressed that while Thaxton and Spencer went off to boarding school, he stayed home. With both of his parents now deceased, he was left in their wake with the Scottish estate he so prized—and a mound of debt.

"I have not been here in a long time," he said, as they traversed the path. The wind carried a strain of violin, a tuning curled into the fabric of the air. Cassandra fell silent for a moment, letting Miles go through memories in his mind. She wondered what he was thinking, her mind full of questions she did not raise. Could they learn to love each other? What would a future with this man really look like? A tightness began in her chest.

"I think I hear Eliza," she said, starting down the path toward her friend's voice, which she thought was coming from the Rose Arena. Eliza was quite fussy about referring to specific areas of the gardens by their proper names. Cassandra barreled forward. If Miles was going to woolgather without explanation, she was not going to waste her time with him.

She could feel him following along behind, albeit at a stroll. Something was on his mind, and it was not she. Cassandra wound her way down the path, relieved that their forced conversation had stalled, although she was stuck on the thread of Spiritualism. If there were people who could talk to ghosts, she and Thaxton could get to the bottom of the wailing woman they'd heard.

Rounding a corner into the Rose Arena, she caught the end of an exclamation.

". . . and if you think that, then the rumors about you are true!"

She found Eliza, talking to Thaxton, with a look of incredulity radiating from under her vast hat brim. Her tone, though teasing, was pointed.

"She heard it, too," Thaxton insisted, indicating Cassandra with a nod of his head as she rounded the corner. "Tell them, Miss Seton."

"I . . . er, yes." Cassandra felt Miles looming behind her, standing too close. She implored Thaxton with her eyes to say no more. "Yes, I heard the noises. Lord Thaxton and I crossed paths in the hallway while we were both searching for the source."

"In the middle of the night?" Eliza asked in a measured tone.

"After midnight," Thaxton said, looking pleased to have been validated, even at potential ruin to Cassandra's reputation.

"That will not do," Miles said, offended. "Wandering around the halls in dishabille is not the way I wish my future wife to conduct herself."

Cassandra pursed her lips, looking up at his stern face. "It is not a habit. I heard a noise."

"It sounded exactly like a woman caterwauling," Thaxton said. "I am not mad, and Miss Seton will vouch for it."

"I will?"

"You did. Now, Percival, do you believe me?"

"Thax," Spencer groaned, "my house is not haunted."

"Spence, I know the place the same as you, and it is bloody well haunted."

Miles interjected. "There is a way to find out for sure."

Cassandra had forgotten he was there again, behind her. The man she would marry. What kind of a picture did they make to the Spencers and Thaxton? What was the expression on his face? He did sound more animated now than when he was trying to explain away his time in Scotland.

"What way?" Thaxton asked.

"Cassandra and I were just discussing this," Miles said. "The spiritual world is accessible to some, but it takes a rare person to tap into it. Someone special, who can perform a ritual to see if Spencer House is host to spirits. It is quite the spectacle, done in drawing rooms across the kingdom. A perfect way to solve the conundrum of your ghost. I knew a few of these adepts in Scotland, and there happens to be one in London as we speak. She could help us."

Finally, he sounded passionate about something.

"This is preposterous," Eliza said. "Absolutely not. We are not doing an evil ceremony at my first house party. No."

"They call it a séance," Miles said. "And it is not evil, Countess. I think it is very nearly a science."

"What does it involve?" Spencer asked with caution, though his curiosity was piqued; it showed in his eyes. He had always said that he never could let an adventure pass him by, even if it seemed like it could end badly. That had not stopped upon his marriage, but now he dragged his wife along with him. Cassandra thought Eliza's resistance formed part of the game between the two, part of the reason they clicked. Eliza protested; Spencer prodded. Not many people dared to tell the Earl Spencer he was wrong; Eliza had never hesitated to do so.

Cassandra stole a glance at Thaxton, whose gaze she had been pointedly avoiding. Just as she suspected, his clean-shaven face blinded her. It seemed that everything else faded into the background. Yet she could tell he was tired, newly sober and drained. It told in his eyes, which looked back at her, presently velvet-textured gray. Highlights of the night before instantly sprang into her mind. The corner of his mouth twitched up ever so slightly. Was someone saying something? Yes. Miles. Miles was talking.

". . . and then she may go into a trance."

Damn. She had missed something important.

"You should write her posthaste," Thaxton said, apparently having retained the power of listening, "and tell her we have a case. Miss Seton and I will be proved irreproachable, and we can put the matter to rest."

"If you two are right about a ghostly visitor," Spencer said, "then I must be wrong. Since the concept of me being wrong is unlikely, let Markwick send for the adept. What can it harm? I thought this house party could use a bit of livening up, anyway."

"Medium, my lord. She calls herself a medium. She's a conduit to the other world. Her name is Lucy Macallister."

It could be that she was imagining things, but Cassandra could swear she heard a note of wistfulness in Miles's voice.

"Prove yourself useful for once, Markwick," Thaxton said, his defiant eyes directed above her head, "and write to Miss Macallister."

Cassandra turned, wanting to see the expression on Miles's face, to see his eyes. There was something in the way he talked about Miss Macallister. As if he was distracted, or fantasizing. At present, though, he was glaring at Thaxton.

"If Lord Spencer bids it," he said, "I will do so. But not because of *your* order."

"I feel as if I should state," said Eliza, "that I think this is a stunningly bad idea."

"Noted," Spencer said. "Miles, why are you still standing there? Go, write."

Cassandra felt Miles lean down. He placed a kiss on the side of her cheek.

"I shall see you as soon as I am done," he said in her ear. "We can finally get some time to ourselves."

Somehow, he made it sound like a threat. Did he mean to kiss her, she wondered, at the same time she saw Thaxton glowering at them? Miles pulled away, leaving a rush of air to fill his place.

"I should have the blue parlor set up to accommodate this . . . séance," Eliza said, already planning. "I cannot believe we are doing this. Spencer, you must ensure that your family is occupied or in bed during the sitting, I will not be responsible for that."

"I will make sure this is our secret," he said, kissing her on the head.

Spencer and Eliza continued talking, with eyes for only each other. Their conversations sometimes seemed exclusionary to those around them. The two had an insular world, one of which Cassandra had often been jealous. They were a team in everything, tempering and urging each other to fully enjoy life. It was something she desired, but instead she had Miles.

"They have no use for us now," Thaxton said, following her eyes to the couple. He shook his head. "Love is an affliction."

"I agree," Cassandra said, although she was unsure if she did. If it was an affliction, it might be one she wanted to contract, as Spencer and Eliza looked so happy. "Lord Thaxton, I should tell you . . . Miles wants me to stay away from you, and I imagine my stepmother will not approve either."

"I am shocked, Miss Seton," he said, deadpan. "I will try to honor that request. We will have to see each other at the séance, of course. There is a mystery to solve, after all."

"But . . . things—things like breakfast cannot continue to happen," she said.

"As you say. I shan't pretend to like it."

He nodded his head to take his leave, and she dropped a not-entirely-formal curtsy. Cassandra watched him walk away, knowing that instead of avoiding him, she would keep waiting for a glimpse. She had a problem. She was falling for a man, but that man was not Miles Markwick.

⚜

After dinner, Miles took Cassandra for a walk on the balcony, an impressive structure that ran along the length of the entire house. Those with a suite on the fourth floor (mostly family—Spencer, Eliza, and two grand guest rooms, one for the dowager and one for Thaxton) were lucky enough to have windows that opened onto the balcony. Many of the party members had taken to closing out the night by lounging there. As they strolled, they passed laughing groups and little dots of candles in the dusk. Cassandra looked around at the carefree celebration and wondered why she did not feel the same.

"It should take two days or so for Miss Macallister to arrive," Miles said, patting her hand as it rested on his arm. He touched her in an increasingly casual way, and she found she was uncomfortable with it. What he probably meant as a gesture to advance intimacy felt more like a statement of ownership. "I am so glad you seem excited about the prospect."

"Of course I am." She smiled up at him. "House parties can often become tedious, especially with family hovering so near. Miss Macallister's séance will be a welcome distraction."

"She is a singular woman," he said.

It was not precisely jealousy Cassandra felt at his open admiration, but the way he spoke of the woman was curious. Worth noting.

"Do you know her well? Miss Macallister?"

With his face turned to the grounds, the moonlight revealed an expression she could not read. A twitch of his lips provided the only visible reaction he had to the question, yet it was a moment before he answered.

"Her father lives in the village near my estate in Scotland. He has often been a great help to me, from acquiring horses to learning about crops. Miss Macallister is fascinating in her own right, the darling of the village. Everyone wanted her to hold séances for them. I suppose that is why the London Spiritualist Society asked her to work with them—her powers are among those of the greatest living mediums."

"It sounds as if she is an actress, putting on plays. How exciting." She meant it; it sounded thrilling.

"I do hope you are not implying her talents are not real," Miles said. His subsequent grin rang false. "In any case, you shall soon see."

"I am not sure I believe spirits would talk to the living at all," she remarked, her hand still tucked securely in his arm. "But I am eager to find out."

"Cassandra!" A voice rang out a length down the balcony. She squinted. Though it was dark, she could just make out her aunt Arabella waving madly in the warm light spilling through the windows. "I wondered where you were."

"Ara," Cassandra said with a smile, embracing her once they closed the distance and kissing her cheek. "I hoped you would be here."

"A little late." She inclined her head toward her husband, who was inside having a lively conversation with Lady Dorset and a few others. "Mr. Fox insisted we stay in the city for some interminable lecture on the finer points of the telephone."

Arabella, Cassandra's favorite aunt, had married Gerald Fox, a prominent lawyer. Cassandra had always loved spending time with her mother's sister, though it had been scarcer since the marquess had married his second wife. Though Arabella was too polite to say it outright, Cassandra suspected that she did not like Lady Dorset at all.

"Mrs. Arabella Fox," Cassandra said, "this is my fiancé, Miles Markwick."

"Oh, yes." Arabella smiled. "We have heard so much about you. I know your father was a great friend of Lord Dorset. My sympathies on his passing."

"Thank you." He bowed his head. "Time is the only thing that makes it better. And happily, it spurred me to reunite with Cassandra. It is a pleasure to meet you, Mrs. Fox."

"Call me Arabella—you will soon be family." She took Cassandra's arm like a schoolgirl, steering her inside. "Come then, both of you. Lady Dorset will be taking her leave soon, as will most of us elders."

"You cannot be more than thirty." Miles smiled.

Arabella laughed at his sudden flattery. She squeezed Cassandra's arm. "Handsome and smart, that one. A good match, I think, for our feisty Cassandra."

A fire burned in the big, open parlor Countess Spencer had designated for mixing in the evening. Some groups played cards, some chatted quietly, others loudly. Cassandra's eyes automatically scanned for Thaxton, but she did not see him.

"There you are," Lady Dorset said as her stepdaughter approached. She focused her gaze on Cassandra for an instant, before turning to Miles with an approving smile. "Though we see you both have a good excuse for your absence."

"A beautiful evening," Miles said. "As is the company."

Introductions were made all around, handled by Lady Dorset as if Miles were a show pony. Cassandra folded her hands as if paying attention and instead listened to Arabella talking to her husband on the fringes of the crowd. She could have sworn she heard the name Vane.

"Such a shame," Arabella was saying. "I remember the Earl Vane as a rollicking good time at parties. I saw his boy earlier; he's here."

"Poor Thaxton," Gerald Fox said. "The whole matter is regrettable."

"Regrettable?" Lady Dorset cut in. "Madness is not regrettable, it just is. It needs to be controlled. Rightly, that man should be locked up so that he cannot hurt anyone. It is foolish of the viscount to take care of him."

"I quite agree," Miles said.

"That is a bit uncharitable," Cassandra said. "We cannot judge something so personal, or know what is best for their family."

Arabella nodded in silent agreement.

Lady Dorset leaned into Cassandra to hide her tone, pulling her aside as she always did when displeased.

"You are quick to defend that man. He is a pariah, and you should not be even remotely interested in him."

"I am not . . ."

"Hush, Cassandra. I am tired. Merely mark me that you are not to align yourself with him."

The warning rang in her head the rest of the night. Should she heed it or not?

Chapter Three

Days passed before they heard from Lucy Macallister, days in which Thaxton honored Miss Seton's request for distance. He went riding with Spencer, attended picnics with the earl's extended family, and attempted to be civilized. When asked about his father, he smiled tightly and lied through his teeth. He cut his normal whisky intake in half, a difficult feat when he had to spend meals at the opposite end of the table from Miss Seton. Looking over and seeing her with Miles, while the lout blathered on in attempts to influence and engage people, made Thaxton want to drink. Profoundly.

On the second night, he did. He gave in to the despair again, because even partial sobriety was making reality too real. A letter arrived from London, his secretary of affairs informing him that all was well at home, but it brought no comfort. Thaxton drank himself into a perfect stupor and fell asleep in an armchair, fully clothed, thinking of how Miss Seton's eyes kept darting to him and then away.

He awoke the next morning, head pounding. Sutton, the valet Spencer had assigned, pushed a mug toward him with a disapproving eye.

"Drink this, my lord." He set a silver platter down next to the mug. "Sulfate of iron, magnesia, peppermint water, and spirit of nutmeg. It will taste repugnant, but serve its purpose. And you have a note."

"I will not be going down for breakfast, Sutton," he said, sitting up with a great deal of effort. "Perhaps not lunch either."

"I will send your regrets."

Thaxton pulled the mug toward him. One sniff told him it was the same evil brew he had drunk the morning of Miles's arrival, so it was best to get it over with—the mixture worked despite tasting abominable. He held his nose and gulped it down.

The note, which he expected was from Spencer, lay folded neatly and unsealed. He snatched it and leaned back in the chair, unbuttoning his waistcoat and letting loose the sigh he had been keeping in while Sutton was in the room. Sutton disapproved of sighing. It mattered little—Thaxton was going to be useless today, elixir or no, and he was considering packing his trunks and leaving. For Spencer's sake, he had tried, but it was not going to work. The current circumstances created a new form of torture he did not want to endure. He fluttered the note open.

Not Spencer's handwriting. This was decidedly feminine.

Thaxton sat up.

Lord Thaxton,
Miss Macallister will arrive this evening. Spencer asked that I inform you of the gathering at midnight in the blue parlor. I look forward to our being proven correct.
—CMS

Cassandra M. Seton, middle name unknown. It would not kill him to stay one more night, if only in order to be proven right, as the alluring Miss Seton had written in her own hand. Thaxton crawled back into bed and slept away the afternoon.

He awoke again to the smell of a huge meal, neatly laid out on the table in his bedroom. It had to be courtesy of Spencer, bless him—he knew exactly what was needed in a situation like this. Venison and heaps of potatoes, a giant pitcher of water. The note from his friend appeared here under the platter.

A last meal before your humiliation. The ghosts are not real, but Miss Seton is, so do dress appropriately. —S.

Thaxton asked Sutton to press his best evening jacket, a high-collared one that he had not worn in a long time, since he had no reason to.

He skipped dinner, being that he was full from lunch and needed more recovery time. He answered his secretary's letter, tending to tedious bits of business, and read the stack of pamphlets he had been neglecting. He sorted through his father's correspondence, brought for that purpose. Thaxton had to carefully read anything that the Earl Vane intended to send.

Two made him sad: one to Thaxton's aunt Emily in which his father complained of the draft in the house, and one that seemed to be a love letter to an invented paramour. His father's flights of fancy were on the increase, and it often became difficult to tell what he had experienced and what he imagined.

The letter that made him angry, addressed to their solicitor, asked to see a copy of his formal will. *Why would he try to go around me?* Thaxton fumed. *Why wouldn't he just ask?* Further than that . . . why was the Earl Vane thinking about mortality? At times he barely knew he was alive.

Still, it took forever for midnight to come. He allowed himself to be fifteen minutes early, arriving first in the blue parlor.

The alleged wailing ghost could not have picked a more appropriate place. Already atmospheric with all its gauzy blue curtains and ornately carved furniture, the blue parlor benefited from candles and fresh flowers the countess had added. A bell rested under a jar in the middle of the table, likely one of the "bizarre requests" of Lucy Macallister. Spencer had been complaining about such requests since receiving her reply to the invitation, a letter sent directly ahead of her arrival. Miss Macallister stipulated that only six people be present at the séance, though many other guests had shown interest. She did not want to "upset the balance of the material versus the spiritual" or something of the sort. The room would pass inspection; it was suitably unnerving. The flames of the tapers gave the only light, so shadows clung to their mates all around the room. Miss Seton had kissed him near the landscape painting in the corner.

As if summoned by the thought, she came through the door.

"Lord Thaxton?" she asked, while looking around, her eyes adjusting to the glow. "Are we too early?"

"Both eager for validation, it would seem." He pulled out a chair for her, opening up the opportunity for him to preemptively stake out the seat beside her. "How are you faring, Miss Seton?"

"Truthfully?" she whispered, peeking out the door. "I am thinking about running away."

"What a coincidence. So was I. Have you any ideas where to go?"

"Perhaps Ireland. Not that I have the faintest idea how I would accomplish that. Where would *you* go?"

"I was going to go home." He paused. "I do not like being away." For the first time outside of talking to Spencer, he wanted to elaborate. He wanted to tell her everything, to explain to her why he was the way he was. The tide of words was about to wash into reality when Spencer walked through the door with Eliza on his arm. Thaxton appreciated the interruption.

"Are we ready to view beyond the veil?" Spencer said, in what he must have thought was a spooky voice. Thaxton rolled his eyes.

"No need for theatrics, Spence. Miss Macallister will tell us if your house is haunted, I will be vindicated, and then we will all go to bed."

"Or," Eliza said, sitting down on the other side of the table, "nothing happens, Spencer is right, and we mourn the sleep we sacrificed to this foolish game."

Miles entered with a petite blonde woman on his arm. She carried a black valise that looked like a doctor's bag and wore a flowing kimono, orange and red silk rippling as she walked. Miss Lucy Macallister, as she was soon introduced. Thaxton knew many poised ladies, but none so self-assured as Miss Macallister. Her nose, not large but with a decided point, tilted high as she looked around with strange translucent green eyes. She held on to Miles's arm a little too long. Thaxton bowed his head as Miles introduced him with the same venom as always, and Miss Macallister's already thin lips compressed in a smile. She moved through the room as if she knew it by heart, though she could have only been in it once or twice that day. She looked, Thaxton thought, more like a governess than a medium.

"Thank you all for having me," she said, the Scottish lilt lending more gravity to her words. "Before we begin, I must ask if anyone has reservations about what we are to do tonight."

"What *are* we to do tonight, Miss Macallister?" asked Cassandra, with what sounded to Thaxton like a hint of distrust. He should not be thinking of Miss Seton by her first name, but he felt like they were well past mere acquaintance, even if they were no longer allowed to foster a friendship. Their kiss had been deep enough that he could not help but claim the intimacy of her name, even if it was just in his head.

Miles pulled out a chair for Miss Macallister, then seated himself across from her, next to his fiancée. That completed the circle, and Thaxton found that the Misses Macallister and Seton flanked him. He was distinctly glad he had not gone home, for it was going to be an interesting night.

"Do call me Lucy; I cannot abide by all this formality." She leaned over to rummage in her bag, fishing out a mix of rose petals and stones, which she arranged neatly around the bell in the middle of the table.

They must have been significant to her, but Thaxton could find no reason for it. No explanation was offered. He heard Miss Seton mutter something beside him, and he smiled without looking at her. She seemed unimpressed by the props. Though she had expressed openness to the supernatural, it did not seem she was easily convinced. He felt the same way, he realized.

"Lucy, then. Is contact with the spirits solely accomplished by the use of . . . trinkets?"

"Cassandra," Miles scolded. "What Lucy does is scientific, tested and proven, and deserves respect."

"So you have been telling me for days."

"Now then," Thaxton said quickly, to cover the combative tone in Miss Seton's voice. She sounded as if she was on the very verge of her temper. *What must have gone on with Miles? Were they quarreling?* Thaxton dared not let himself hope. "I think we would all feel better if Lucy explained exactly what to expect during the séance."

"Thank you, Lord Thaxton." Lucy folded her hands. "I cleansed the room with sage earlier, so no one need dread demonic presence. From what Miles tells me, we are trying to get in contact with a voice you heard in this room. In that case, I will enter a trance, with everyone's help. We can ask the spirit to show itself and then hopefully ask it yes-or-no questions. The spirits communicate through rapping noises, sometimes using the bell on the table, and rarely . . . through me."

"They talk through you?" Eliza asked, sounding awed.

"I suppose you could say that. They use me; I never remember what goes on when I go under the spell."

Thaxton could hear Miss Seton drumming her fingernails on the table, as if trying to hold herself back from saying something. The way she fidgeted, Thaxton got the impression she was antsy, though he could not pretend to know why. Miles noticed, shooting her a look that tensed up their side of the table. There were a few moments of loaded silence.

"How do we help?" Spencer asked, ever the peacekeeper.

"First, we join hands."

Lucy extended her hands to Spencer and Thaxton. Spencer had already been holding Eliza's, who took Miles's, who then took Miss Seton's. Thaxton looked down at his right hand and Cassandra's left. He was going to be holding hands with Miss Seton. After a moment of expectant hesitation, he curled his fingers around hers.

❧❀☙

Cassandra struggled to maintain a cool expression, as if she were perfectly at ease holding the hands of both her dreary future husband and the gorgeous mess of a viscount. Miles's hand remained limp in hers with an unpleasant clamminess. Thaxton had begun rubbing his gloved thumb lazily against her palm, doing funny things to her composure.

Lucy closed her eyes and sat up straight.

"Please center your thoughts on the spirits who may inhabit this room," she intoned.

Far easier said than done. Cassandra had spent the previous days looking forward to the séance as a beacon of light at the end of a tunnel. Miles had turned obsessed with Scotland and Miss Macallister, capable of reciting hours of useless facts about the landscape and history of the country. He had once even called her a Sassenach. So ridiculous, as if he was not English himself.

Never mind that she spent those days mostly wondering where Lord Thaxton was and looking forward to seeing him at dinner, even if he was scowling at the other end of the spread of food. She sensed that he was having the exact amount of fun that she was at the party; that is to say, none at all. The error of their kiss had done something to her brain, rearranged it in an irreversible way.

"It would help if you closed your eyes," Lucy advised, her own shut tight, her face placid. "I can feel all of your minds wandering."

Though Cassandra did not believe this woman for an instant, she felt she should give it a go. Miles's eyes had fluttered shut along with Spencer's. Eliza looked over at her, lips quirked up to one side. "Nonsense," the countess mouthed before shutting her own eyes gamely. Cassandra felt Thaxton squeeze her hand, and she turned her head ever so slightly to look at him, the one open pair of eyes at the table.

Concentrate? With him next to her?

He smiled and looked away, his lids dropping. She closed her own eyes, though it seemed ridiculous. Yes, she had heard something in this room, but that something was not going to use Lucy as a conduit from the beyond. It was not possible.

"That's better," Lucy said in a softer voice. "Spirits, if you are here, we invite you to be at ease. We mean no harm; we seek confirmation. We would be honored and grateful should you choose to make your presence known."

Cassandra had never heard such a lot of hogwash. If she were a spirit, the last thing she would be doing would be hanging around waiting to talk to Lucy Macallister. An obstinate silence filled the air.

"We invite you to rap on the table if you are here."

More silence, enough that Cassandra was ready to suggest that the experiment had been a failure. A loud rap startled her, and her eyes shot open. Lucy's were shut, but everyone else's eyes had also opened wide. They all exchanged looks.

"Did . . . you?" Spencer asked, addressing all of them at once.

"Lord Spencer, please," Lucy said in a soothing tone. "It is a delicate time. I understand initial contact is rattling, but I know you can all resume concentration. The energy of this group is very powerful. Complete silence, please."

Thaxton's hand went still, no more wandering fingers. His eyes were already shut, and his face had gone tight—did he believe this? Cassandra, aghast, watched the rest of the table close their eyes again, their faces etched with apprehension and fright. Even Eliza had scooted closer to her husband, an arm's length from Miles, who clutched her fingers in a frozen grip.

Cassandra's eyebrows drew together. *They all believed it. What could have come over them?* Eliza, who had been so sure that there could not possibly be supernatural activity in her house, hung on to Percy, actually afraid. Lucy swayed back and forth a bit. Thaxton held the medium's hand with two fingers, whereas he held hers so snugly that she felt his bones moving beneath.

"We sense you, honored spirit," Lucy said, her voice melodramatic. "We thank you for being open to communicate. May we ask you some questions? Rap once for yes, and twice for no. Can you do this for us?"

One solid rap.

Cassandra looked all around the room. Where was it coming from? There was a dumbwaiter in the corner. Did Lucy have an accomplice hiding there? She could not see that far, but it was a strong prospect.

"Are you the spirit whom Miss Seton and Lord Thaxton heard a few nights ago?"

Another knock, a single for yes. Thaxton opened his eyes. Even in the midst of all the lunacy, his perfection took Cassandra aback. Not that he was unflawed, no, but he was everything she would have listed if asked to describe a handsome man. Now with a dreadfully fetching crease of confusion drawing his eyebrows into a straight line.

"Can this be true?" he asked under his breath.

"I sincerely doubt it," she said, not loud enough for Lucy to hear. Miles did, though, and it earned her a harsh "shh." Cassandra frowned. After the miserable past few days, she did not care if he disapproved. He could run off to Scotland with Lucy immediately if he wanted, for all she cared.

Lucy resumed.

"Honored spirit, are you a female, as Miss Seton and Lord Thaxton have indicated?"

Another yes. Thaxton's hand entwined with Cassandra's, holding hands in an affectionate way, not simply to create a circle. Miles remained unmoving and blind. Spencer had rearranged himself so that his arm curved around his wife, her hand tucked against him, the circle unbroken.

"Are you attached to this family?" Lucy asked.

Softly, but certainly, the bell on the table rang once.

"Impossible!" Cassandra exclaimed. She nearly dropped Thaxton's hand.

"Miss Seton. Remain calm."

No one's eyes were closed anymore. She felt Thaxton's knee hit hers under the table. He was fidgeting, like he wanted to dash. Eliza, too, appeared as if she would rather not be in the room.

"Calm," Lucy repeated, her strange dark-green eyes opening slowly. "We are very close to the line between worlds."

Miles's hand felt too warm, and the room felt too quiet. Thaxton's knuckles poked her through the glove; Cassandra worried (not for the first time) that he was not eating enough. She noticed that she thought a lot about his welfare lately.

"If I go into a trance," Lucy said, her voice belabored, pulled out of her, "you must not break the circle. It would be very dangerous."

Cassandra didn't know much about Spiritualism and had never been to a séance before, but she could not believe a spirit actually rang the bell. She had never thought deeply about spirits, but now, she realized she did not believe it possible. She remembered what she had said to Miles earlier about Lucy being like an actress—that was it. The whole thing seemed polished, recited. Very well, yes, but more a play than a phenomenon.

"I am going to invite the spirit to speak through me. In this situation, I need someone else to ask questions. Lord Spencer, if you will?"

Spencer looked a bit surprised to hear his name.

"Certainly," he said uncertainly.

"It is best to ask questions to lead the spirit, focusing on what it may want," Lucy continued. "I implore no one to move in an abrupt manner or disturb the air with other noises." She looked sharply to Cassandra.

"I will behave," Cassandra promised.

"This may not work," Lucy said, "but I think we have a good chance. I can feel the veil shimmering. Now, total concentration, please."

Cassandra did not want to go on with the charade. It was not fun or lighthearted or whimsical. She tensed with all the things she wanted to say, such as *This is balderdash* and *Why don't all of you think this is balderdash?* Lucy's head lolled down, her face shadowed by the half-spent candles, her breathing slowly evening out as the room expanded in anticipation.

"Good evening," Lucy said in a voice flat and unaccented.

"Spirit?" Spencer croaked, startled to hear the words, somewhere between skepticism and outright fear. "Is that what I should call you?"

"That is not important."

Lucy smiled, but it was not friendly. Her eyes had glazed over; her face took on a reptilian cast. The smile itself brought to mind a snake.

"Can we help you in any way?" Spencer asked, as if to a visiting villager.

"I have a message," Lucy said. She stared into the flame of a nearby candle as if it contained the answers of all life. "It is for the thirteenth earl."

"Ah. I am the ninth," Spencer said, sounding pleased that he was not the recipient of a message from the beyond.

"Me," Thaxton said hoarsely. "She means me. I will be the thirteenth Earl Vane when my father passes. I am the thirteenth earl."

Cassandra tightened her hand. Thaxton was faltering. He was as pale as . . . as a ghost, though that metaphor was fraught.

"This is silly," she said, attempting to inject reason.

Miles, who fancied himself an expert on the process, tugged on her hand. "Cassandra. Please. Your belief is not necessary, but refrain from being insulting." He tried to make eye contact with Lucy, but she stared stalwartly off into the air.

"Honored spirit," Miles continued while Cassandra simmered at his behavior. "What is this message you have for Lord Thaxton?"

"Jonathan Aubrey Vane, Viscount Thaxton," Lucy intoned, tilting her head toward the viscount. Cassandra felt coiled beside him. "Thirteenth Earl Vane. Heed me. Your father is mad, as his father before him, as you shall be, unless you break the curse. It rests on your head. You know your fate, Jonathan Aubrey; you have always known. Do what you must."

"How?" Thaxton rasped. "How do I break it?"

"End your family line," Lucy said in that hollow voice, turning Thaxton's hand over and peeling off his glove. Cassandra felt an unfounded fury at the way Lucy was touching him. She placed two fingers on his palm, pausing for a painful moment before drawing a big breath. "Be the last Vane to hold the title."

Thaxton was looking down at her hand like it was on fire, his blue-gray eyes huge, and shades darker than a moment before.

"Die," Lucy finished, her voice a growl. "Die and break the curse."

She began shuddering, and Thaxton snatched his hand away, breaking the circle. His white glove dropped from Lucy's grip and floated to the floor. The medium wavered, near-faint, but not before Miles could catch her, cradling her to the ground. Her eyes rolled back in her head and then fluttered shut.

Thaxton was on his feet a second later, his arms out to his sides in a contained state of agitation. Cassandra caught him by the cuff.

"Stop," she said. "Wait, wait. This is—"

"No," he said. "No, no, good night."

With that, he turned on his heel and left the room. Panic finally hit Cassandra, after seeing the look on Thaxton's face when he fled the parlor. Seeing him scared made her scared. Lucy was in a full swoon, with Eliza waving smelling salts under her nose.

"She is breathing," Eliza said with relief.

Lucy, entirely wreathed in Miles's embrace on the floor, opened her eyes. Spencer stood, crossing toward Cassandra through the chaos of the medium's pronouncement.

"Go," he said under his breath. "Go after him. We will sort things out here. He goes to the library when he is upset."

"I couldn't possibly," she said, the words spilling out too quickly, devoid of truth. She wanted nothing more than to go after him.

"Before they realize you are gone, Miss Seton—go."

Chapter Four

Thaxton barreled blindly down the hall, leaving the disarray of the séance behind him. He could hear some guests still on the balconies, their laughter filtering down. The merriment only served to drive home the point that he was doomed.

The library had a convenient stock of superior alcohol and a cocoon of utmost solitude—it was his favorite place in Spencer House. The walls, lined with bookshelves, spines of all colors below high windows, the moving ladder to reach the highest tomes, antique clocks under glass to keep out everyday dust, solid wooden furniture that had to be ancient—it all somehow added up to a feeling of security. He poured himself a drink and lay down on the settee, balancing the glass on his torso. He thought he might drink himself to death, if that was what the earldom wanted from him. His duty, as earl, would be to die. This was not news to him. It was exactly as his father and now the séance had prophesized—he would be the one to end it.

Spencer had always said there was no solid evidence of the Vane family curse. He thought the "curse," which he only talked about in quotation marks, was a construct of coincidence and hallucination.

Thaxton did not feel the same—he felt distinctly imperiled, waiting to go mad. It was no way to live a life.

And in that case, why bother? He put the glass on his forehead, the cool crystal making a halo. If this was his destiny, then so be it. It was not as if he had much to live for, anyway. Maybe he would swan-dive off a balcony. That would be fairly no-muss; it could even look like an accident.

"Lord Thaxton?"

"Go away, Cassandra," he said, realizing too late that he had used her familiar name.

She stepped into the library and closed the door behind her.

"Spencer sent me," she said. "To check on you."

"Very manipulative of him," Thaxton said, "but I do not want to talk. You can tell Spencer I am well, and you may go."

She advanced to the settee until she loomed over him. He did not know what hurt worse, her loveliness or the actual concern in her eyes.

"No, Jonathan." He should not have opened the door to Christian names, for his coming out of her mouth had an odd effect on him. She sounded breathless; she must have run. "Though the earl may have granted me leave, I am not here on his account, but by my own volition. That woman, Lucy, is lying. I just feel it, and we have to prove it. Do not tell me you believe this farce."

"She knew things I have not told anyone but Spencer, things my father has said in the grip of madness. Think of me what you will, Miss Seton, but I leave on the morrow. It is time for me to go home."

She sat on the edge of the settee, pushing his legs over.

"Cassandra," she corrected. "Or Cassie. Whichever you prefer. I find that they both suit on different occasions."

"Hmm," Thaxton said, sitting up a bit more and taking a long drink, which he felt he deserved for his restraint. He hoped that reply invited no further conversation.

"I do not want you to go home," she said bluntly.

"Being that you are engaged to another man, I do not think what you want is any of my business."

"If you wish to pretend you do not care what I want, I will not shatter your illusion."

"Please go to bed," he said, placing the tumbler against his forehead again. "I have nothing to say, no witty banter, no assurances, no hope. And no energy to pretend otherwise."

"No need to pretend anything. Thaxton, I am certain that woman is a fake. Please, stop and think about this. You said she echoed things your father has said—what do you mean exactly, and would he tell anyone else?"

He had noticed her eyes flickered with disapproval every time he drank. He took another sip before answering in order to irritate her.

"My father," he said, pointing a finger out from the lip of the cup, "talks to me and his roses, and no one else. He did not even register Spencer the last time he was in town."

He was not sure why he had told her that. It was too personal; Thaxton had not even discussed it with Spencer because they were both so shaken by it. Damn this woman and the strange need he had to confess to her.

"In circumstances like these," she said, "I like to reassure the person in pain that I know how they feel. But I will not lie to you, Jonathan. I have no idea what that must feel like. I doubt anyone does."

"I would not expect you to," he said, feeling a bit more charitable as the alcohol warmed him. "I do not want you to know what this feels like."

"I know you do not want to talk," she said, balancing her words as if they were spinning plates, "and I do not want to pry. But what happened in there upset all of us, and I cannot leave you to your devices."

"'Upset' seems an understatement," he said, motioning for her to hand him the whisky decanter. She did so, but with reservation. "I was told that I am a marked man. Although, to be frank, it is not the first time."

"So. Your father also said that you had to die to break the curse."

"Not exactly, but close enough." Thaxton leaned over, spinning the stand-up globe slowly, not wanting to look at her. "He insists that I am chosen to put an end to the calamity that is our family line. Sometimes he cautions me to never marry and to remain childless. He never said I had to die, though. That is a new development."

"Lies, I'm sure." Cassandra seethed. She seemed certain that Lucy Macallister was a fraud. Thaxton knew it was not as simple as that. As he saw it, Lucy was a channel of confirmation. He poured himself another glass, since it did not matter what Miss Seton thought of him—he did not have anything to offer her. He felt condemned.

"What good would going home do?" she pressed on. "What would it accomplish? You would be alone, confused, terrified, and worrying around your father. Stay here, Jonathan, where we can make sense of it."

He expelled a bitter laugh.

"You propose to make sense of a problem that had plagued me most of my adult life?"

"We will start with the séance. Certainly there have to be clues as to how Miss Macallister performs the ruse."

"Lucy," he said into his glass. "She hates formality; call her Lucy."

"How long have you been tippled, Lord Thaxton?" Her look of censure returned. "And I do not mean tonight. I mean, how long have you been keeping this ludicrous amount of alcohol running through you daily?"

"This much?" He had to stop and think in order to answer honestly. "A few weeks. Since Spencer was last in London."

"When your father did not recognize him."

"Yes. I find it much easier to drink than to process the implications of that."

Thaxton took another long pull, but this one was primarily to stop the words that wanted to come out of his mouth: *Because if he doesn't remember Spencer, then how long before he forgets me? And then how long until I am the damned thirteenth Earl Vane?*

"Consider staying," she said with those irksome sympathetic eyes. "Do not make me investigate alone."

"Miles should help you. I am quite busy dying, my lady."

"Miles idolizes Lucy. I do not think I can count on him in this."

Thaxton canted his head, ignoring the seasickness the sudden action caused. "Miles idolizes the medium?" The possibility was promising—if that were so, maybe he was in love with her and might leave Cassandra. The thought of their marriage sickened Thaxton.

"Truly. Lucy Macallister and Spiritualism are his topics of conversation, like an obsessed convert. I cannot marry him."

"No," Thaxton answered automatically, again into his glass. "Anyone but him. Or myself. You could not possibly marry me. Good lord, not me."

Her charity for him vanished instantly. His mistake sounded so boorish in hindsight. The drink had loosened his tongue, and honestly, he felt so comfortable with her that he lost track of his thoughts, saying things aloud that he should keep to himself. He had not meant it the way she took it. That much was obvious as she rose from the settee.

"No, Cassandra—I did not mean I find you lacking," he began, hauling himself unsteadily to his feet. "Or that I do not . . ."

"I understand, Lord Thaxton."

"What I should say is that—what I mean is, I will never marry, not you especially. I cannot put—"

She raised her hand, the very one he had been holding earlier that evening. It had felt very nice during the séance, but now it was inches from his face in full censure. "I said I understand, my lord. It is very late; I should go to bed. You ought to retire as well, if you mean to leave on the morrow."

He stopped short of reaching out for her, which she definitely would not have welcomed. "Cassandra—"

She turned back, as if it were an effort to do so. "Please, do not apologize. I should be begging your forgiveness. It was too bold of me to try to help you. If you want to believe in nonsense, it is your prerogative. I bid you a safe trip back to London."

Miss Cassandra Seton had the best flounce Thaxton had ever witnessed, a sharp turn out of the room with a hint of haughtiness. His first instinct was to go after her and pull her into his arms. Instead, he sank back onto the settee, his drink sloshing all over it.

He had offended her, he knew. But she had misunderstood—he could not marry anyone, as he had tried to clarify. The thought of sentencing another person, especially her, to a life with him was deplorable. He had no future; why would he drag Cassandra, full of anima and vibrancy, into that?

But he wanted her. She deserved far better, yet he wanted her. He sank deeper into the cushions, allowing his tired eyes to close. The complicated world could fall into oblivion for a few blessed hours, but it would all still be there tomorrow—the family curse, the talking spirits, the beautiful but inconvenient woman.

It would all be there tomorrow.

❧❀❧

Cassandra opened her eyes the next morning, and nothing had changed. She still did not want to marry Miles, still felt Lucy was running some kind of game, still felt drawn to Thaxton although it was now evident that he did not feel the same.

A letter from her father lay on her desk, sending his regards and the news that the banns would be read in their parish in preparation for the marriage of one Miss Cassandra Seton to one Mr. Miles Markwick. Seeing their names linked together thusly turned her stomach. She tore the letter into little pieces as she drank her tea, swaddled again in a robe. Would it be better to run away or to face this head-on? She considered replying to her father with a heartfelt plea to be released from the obligation, but only for a moment. That would never work. To her parents, her marriage to Miles honored a business arrangement.

Her entire future, to fulfill a debt to Miles's deceased father.

She needed to talk out her confusion, so she sought out Eliza before breakfast.

"Good morning, dear," the countess said, fluttering around while arranging the last details of the special morning meal. Lucy, having recovered, had agreed to speak on Spiritualism to the assembled ladies, who were buzzing with interest, having learned of her background.

Cassandra tried not to look dejected.

"So?" Eliza folded her hands.

"So . . ."

"Spencer told me he sent you to comfort Thaxton."

"That was what he sent me to do? Then I was unsuccessful."

"Not as I understand it. Spencer fully expected the viscount to flee back to London, but instead he arrived early for breakfast. Downstairs, even. He was terribly bedraggled, though."

"Oh?" she said noncommittally. "I am glad he is well, then. What of Lucy? How does she fare?"

"Lucy is fine. She does not remember anything, and she remains very shaken. I have asked her to stay on for the rest of the party. Do not give me that look, Cassandra; it would have been impolite to send her away."

"You are right. Besides, I would rather her be near, as it will make it easier for me to figure out exactly what happened last night. I do not think she is as innocent as she appears."

"Do as you must, but try not to ruin my house party. Have mercy on me, darling. Spencer's whole family is here, and I am the unsure new countess."

"I will be the very picture of discretion," Cassandra swore.

"What are you going to do about Miles?" Eliza asked, pulling on her loose braid. She was trying to be casual, Cassandra noted, which was sweet of her, but unnecessary. She did not feel the least bit slighted at Miles's disinterest in her. They were so poorly matched that it was laughable.

"I do not know. I was too distracted to think, due to Thaxton's breakdown."

"He had a breakdown?"

"He is currently having one, and I suspect it has been going on for some time. Even if he seems well this morning."

"Cassie," Eliza said, suspicion coloring her words, "you seem far more concerned with Lord Thaxton than Miles."

"It is nothing," she said quickly.

"I knew it!" Eliza exclaimed. "I knew there was something going on with you two. Spencer said he did not know, but he had this mischievous twinkle in his eye. Tell me."

"There was . . . there was a small, inconsequential kiss."

"I *knew* it," the countess said triumphantly.

"But I swear nothing will come of it. He has made it very clear that it was a mistake. He was foxed."

"How very intriguing." Eliza grinned, starting to move toward the door as ladies filtered in. "You must tell me more later."

Aunt Arabella entered with Lady Dorset in tow. Lady Beatrice Valentine, whom Cassandra and Eliza had hated in finishing school, accompanied them. The girl, an atrocious gossip, had won Lady Dorset's favor.

"Good morning," she chirped as she sat down. "I am so looking forward to hearing Miss Macallister speak."

Cassandra nodded mutely, for that was the very opposite of how she felt. Lucy glided into the room, making the rounds in a conspicuous order of hierarchy. She started with the countess, and Cassandra couldn't help but watch her face as Lucy fed Eliza whatever story she had memorized about the night before.

Beatrice's maid had piled her straight hair atop her head using clips adorned with dragonflies. The sparkling green gems of the barrettes stood out garishly against her pale blonde coif. They had been in the same class at Cheltenham, though Bea had done much more talking than learning.

"I heard Miss Macallister knows your fiancé, Cassandra. What an interesting man you are marrying—why, Miles was just telling me at dinner last night how important Spiritualism is to him."

"Yes," Cassandra said. "He is a most thoughtful man. Intellectually curious." She didn't think that was exactly true, but it sounded good.

Lucy, after her promenade of introductions, crossed to the front of the room. Arabella passed a tray to Cassandra, full of various confections, and the look on her aunt's face shone as if she were at the theater. It seemed Lucy Macallister's talents had become the talk of the house party, though thankfully it did not seem rumors of what actually happened at the séance had spread.

"Thank you all for your kindness and for making me feel welcome here," Lucy said. "It is a testament to the goodness of your Christian souls that you would be hospitable to a stranger. And our beliefs align—contrary to what you might think, Spiritualists are not godless heathens. Just the opposite! We believe our faith is so strong that we are allowed a window into the beyond. That window comes in the form of séances and sometimes automatic writing, which those blessed with the gift can perform. We access the spirits directly, and they speak through us."

"It sounds ghastly," Beatrice said, with a dramatic shiver.

"Not at all, Lady Beatrice. I understand that a séance can be a scary prospect, but they are key to the study of the afterlife, which faith demands. The spirits have much to teach us, if we let them in."

"I shall leave that to you." Beatrice giggled, and Cassandra gave her a stern look. Though Lucy was not her favorite person, she didn't deserve to be interrupted.

Lucy laughed, though not as girlishly. Nothing so coy with her. Her laugh spoke of experience.

"Yes, that is a common reaction. But I see my mediumship as a gift; I am a steadfast steward of it."

"Is it terribly dangerous?" Arabella asked with sincere worry.

"For a novice, perhaps," Lucy said. "I myself have been developing my gift since adolescence, and there is no danger at my tables."

"Is it . . ." Lady Dorset lowered her voice and paused, searching for the right word. "Demonic?"

Lucy's laugh rang out again, a musical tinkle. "Heavens no, Lady Dorset. Bless your heart, no. There is nothing demonic in my practice, though there have been documented cases. We must ever be on the watch for evil."

"Some people say it is a parlor trick."

Lucy's head turned to Cassandra. "A sad and unfair dismissal, Miss Seton."

Cassandra took a long sip of her tea, silent.

Lucy looked back at the rest of the group, not losing a bit of composure. She moved on quickly, and no one marked Cassandra's comment or pushed it further.

"I am happy to answer any questions you might have. If you want further study, I have both literature and recommendations. After the house party, I will be returning to London to study with the London Spiritualist Society and would welcome a visit from any of you esteemed ladies. I would be happy to start you on a journey of discovery."

Cassandra was not interested in any such journey, but many of the ladies were. They broke into groups of excited chatter, Beatrice tugging on Lucy's sleeve like an excited child trying to curry favor. Cassandra shuddered to think that Bea could become a protégée.

She was about to excuse herself when a servant approached her with a tray. She took the note off it and thanked him, hoping against hope that Miles was not requesting her presence somewhere.

The compact and elegant handwriting was not Miles's; his was a hasty scrawl. This trim and neat hand said:

Labyrinth R, L, L, R, L.

"Excuse me," she said, setting her napkin on the table. The ladies must have stared at her haste, but she was not there to see it. If her hunch was correct, the note consisted of directions to meet in the garden labyrinth, and as Miles hadn't the imagination to think of something like that, it could only be one person.

She rushed along the green, fertile hallways, occasionally checking the note to be sure of her rights and lefts. After a particularly long stretch that she thought must put her somewhere near the middle, she made her last left turn into the very center of the labyrinth.

A tall fountain cascaded. It was cool, the place shaded by the tall hedges, which grew taller in the center. The only sounds came from the water and birds, unsullied by anything else. The place felt like a sanctuary, like a sort of holy ground, walled from the outside world. Thaxton sat on one of the benches that surrounded the fountain, his back to her, lounging on his palms. The sun on his profile when he tilted his head made it more apparent how pale he was, how he had wilted by hiding himself away.

"Did you sleep at all?" she asked by way of greeting.

"A little," he said, turning around. His eyes shone surprisingly vibrantly for a man who must be practically pickled on the inside by now. "I am so glad you came. I thought you might not."

"My curiosity gets the better of me. And I intend to investigate the medium, so I could not risk the chance you have information that would help me."

The explanation sounded so logical and thorough. Cassandra was proud of herself. It gave no hint of the real reason she had come, which was that she was always desperately wanting to see him, and she could not say why. Especially after the awkwardness of the night before.

"I want to be a part of the investigation," he said, patting the bench beside him. "I do not have any new information, but I have thought it over, and it would be ungentlemanly to let you undergo such a thing alone."

"I am sure I can manage without you," she said, not sitting but standing beside the bench. He yanked her arm, tugging her down so that they sat with knees touching. She thought he would move over to make room, but he did not. The fabric of his dark-gray trousers remained against the lace trim of her skirt in the warm sun. The small amount of contact felt strangely intimate, even more so when he took her hand.

"I am sure you can. I *want* to help you. But first you must forgive me," he said, his eyes locked on hers. He looked so solemn; it made her shift uneasily. "I misspoke last night; it was idiocy. I do not think you unmarriageable—quite the opposite. I meant that I would be the worst choice of a husband for you."

"Thaxton," she said, feeling a great need to stop him, "I think it best that we avoid topics like this."

"Do you forgive me?" he pressed. "Additionally, do you forgive me for being a boor, being soused, being loutish, et cetera? I need you to forgive me now, for I will do it again in the future, and I want to be sure you will forgive me then."

"I have changed my mind, Jonathan. I think you might in fact already be mad."

"Unkind," he said, shaking his head.

"I forgive you."

"Capital. Now then, have you a plan to prove your theory about the supernatural mistress?"

"I thought I would start by investigating the séance room. There had to be some way she was causing the rapping and the bell. And now that you are involved, it would behoove us to write your father and ask him if he has had any unexpected visitors lately. Of the Scottish variety."

"I do not see how . . ."

"You said Lucy knew things that only your father would know. We cannot rule out that she somehow tricked him."

"Yes, true. We should investigate the séance room sometime during the ball tonight, when everyone will be occupied. Put me on your dance card for the second waltz."

"You do remember that Miles asked me to avoid you."

"Indeed I do." The viscount broke into a roguish smile, getting up from the bench and backing slowly into the labyrinth, a spring in his step. "What a pity we shall have to defy him."

Chapter Five

Thaxton spent the rest of the day catching glimpses of a miserable Cassandra, being dragged around by Miles, who was being dragged around by Lucy. The countess could not extract her friend, busy as she was with the preparations for the ball, made even larger than usual by attendees from the village that surrounded Spencer House. Maids and footmen clogged the hallways arranging, fetching, and often upending the items they carried. To Thaxton, it was dizzying. The whisky he had set on the floor of the library had remained there, untouched. He had not even taken off the top of the decanter to steal a whiff.

Reality, as it leaked back in, was not welcoming.

"So," Spencer prodded, seemingly into the center of Thaxton's headache, "you begged her forgiveness?"

"You make it sound so unpleasant. I acknowledged that I was acting like an ass."

Though, now that he examined it, it was possible that he had been begging her. Only a bit. A touch. A negligible amount of begging.

They were in the earl's bedroom, getting ready to descend for the ball. Spencer's room was all dark wood furniture, masculine and imposing, with a line of stained-glass half windows on the wall that faced the grounds. Since his marriage, there were always signs of Eliza's presence—a stray hairbrush here, an abandoned brooch there. They kept separate rooms, technically, but they did not sleep apart.

"Hand me that pin," Spencer said, adjusting his formal white tie. "I cannot recall you apologizing, Jonathan. For anything. Ever."

"What are you implying?"

"Nothing, nothing." Spencer grasped his forearm in a gesture of affection. "It does not matter why you stayed, just that you did. You have a habit of running from difficult situations."

"This particular difficult situation cannot be ignored." Thaxton fingered the delicate gold embroidery around the outside of his waistcoat. Elaborate work for an embellishment hardly anyone would notice. He stopped himself before he could follow that metaphor.

"The spirits or Miss Seton?"

"Both." Thaxton pulled on his tailcoat, taking a moment to tug the bottom before buttoning it. He had let Sutton pin and prod him the day before to make adjustments, and the black velvet now fit like a glove. He put his hand on the doorknob to start downstairs, but a thought struck. He looked back at Spencer.

"I notice Lucy Macallister has joined our party. Am I to infer that you think she's telling the truth about . . . everything?"

"Absolutely not. Last night's performance, though convincing, could not have been real. I personally think she's having an affair with Miles. But Eliza thinks it would be poor mannered to boot her out."

Spencer had the exact same thoughts as Miss Seton. Thaxton's opinion of Miles's fiancée deepened. As they descended the long staircase that led to the grand ballroom, the assembled crowd filtered from a mass of color to distinguishable shapes. Thaxton told himself he was looking for Cassandra because they needed to plan their exploration and not because he wanted to see what she was wearing. He did hope that her fashion tastes ran toward the gowns that dipped scandalously low in the front.

Sobriety was also bringing back his libido in full force. Just imagining that Miss Seton might dare such a frock forced him to discreetly adjust his coat, else risk undue attention.

Eliza scooped up Spencer immediately and took him to the front to greet guests as they arrived. Thaxton found himself on his own, which was a small miracle at events like these. People streamed in at a steady pace, glittering in the mass of candles blazing, reflecting off every surface. He smiled to himself and ducked behind a marble pedestal to avoid running into Lady Desmond, who knew his father and would have commanded his ear for an hour had she seen him.

Near the orchestra, Lucy Macallister laughed up at Miles Markwick, who evidently had said something worthy of a laugh for the first time in his life. Lucy's ball gown had three collars, a petticoat of white silk, and a generously ruffled overskirt. Cassandra stood next to them sullenly, drinking a glass of champagne, looking as if she would commit murder to be anywhere else.

She was indeed wearing one of the gowns he had imagined. A flattering midnight blue with a square-cut bodice, deep enough to satisfy his visions. Viscount Thaxton, never known to approach any group of people, headed straight for them.

"Good evening, all," he said, sliding in between Miles and Lucy's conversation. The relief on Cassandra's face was apparent, her eyebrows shooting together gratefully.

"Lord Thaxton," she said, their eyes locking for a moment, their secret a charge between them. "Good evening."

"Dragged yourself out of bed, I see," Miles said.

"I did not want to disappoint you, Markwick. And good evening, Lucy. How nice that the earl extended the invitation."

"Oh, indeed," she said, as if she had expected just that. "My trunks will arrive on the morrow. I am so grateful to the Spencers and welcome the opportunity to rest, as I spend most of my time teaching about Spiritualism. It is rather exhausting."

"I am sure," Cassandra said, a clipped sentence that held so much more meaning than length.

"While we are on the subject," Thaxton said, feeling a developing rhythm between him and Cassandra, "I do hope you are recovered from the horror of last night."

"Is this sort of thing a regular occurrence in your line of work?" Cassandra asked. Thaxton realized that they had arranged themselves opposite Lucy like interrogators, without being aware of it.

"Being a medium is not an occupation, my dear; it is a calling."

"Yes, but does it? Happen often, the trance?" Thaxton prompted.

"I want to make it clear, Lord Thaxton, that I do not remember things when I go under. I was told our session was particularly brutal, and I am sorry. I understand if you are feeling . . . emotionally confused."

Thaxton felt a great surge of irritation. Cassandra bristled beside him.

"You have not answered the question," she said.

Lucy's eyes narrowed. "I covered this at the séance. Perhaps you were not paying attention. I said it happens rarely."

Miles touched Lucy's arm, and Thaxton bit back his disgust with the man. He was not even trying to hide the strong attraction between him and the medium. Miles and Cassandra were not a good match, but the man should be a bit more discreet.

"You must excuse Lucy," Miles said, attempting to calm ruffled feathers. "She deals a lot with suspicion, and it begins to wear on the soul. Surely, Thaxton, you can sympathize with people doubting your word."

For the first time that day, Thaxton's fingers itched for a glass.

"Your wit has improved, Miles," he said. "Must be the Scottish air."

The orchestra was starting up as the room filled. Thaxton pushed down the urge he had to whisk Cassandra away and introduce her to his family. That was an impossible fancy, to put it mildly, considering that not many of them were present. Besides that, she was engaged to someone else, and he had never introduced a woman to his family. Not in the way he wanted to introduce Cassandra. Perhaps she might have already met some of them, since they were related to Miles as well. Anyone he could have personally introduced her to probably already knew her through Miles, and his father was in London, safe.

He snuck a peek at Cassandra's dance card, hanging from her wrist. Her first waltz as well as the dinner dance that led into the meal were consigned to Miles. She had left the second waltz open, as they had discussed. He would have to fix that. There were some names he did not recognize, for a quadrille and a galop, a dance he hated. He found that he did not like that, seeing other men's names on her dance card.

"Miss Seton," he said, careful with his formality in the ballroom. "Honor me with the second waltz?"

Miles and Lucy had returned to their private conversation, something about a lecture that she was going to give at the London Spiritualist Society. Thaxton picked up Cassandra's wrist to access her dance card, haunting the inside of her palm far too long, his fingers caressing her. For a moment, the dance invitation had nothing to do with their investigation.

He picked up the pencil attached to the card and scrawled his name. He had a passing fancy to extend the *X* all the way down the lines, to claim every last remaining dance, something that was nigh impossible.

Thaxton dropped the card and her wrist reluctantly. This was getting dangerous; he was having human feelings.

He excused himself, knowing that any more contact with Miss Seton would be noticed. Even at a private country house party, there were people who would spread rumors with glee. If he showed her much more favor, London would know within the week that the Ghost was courting the Marquess of Dorset's daughter.

Wait, he stopped himself. *Am I courting her?*

That would be patently absurd. He could not court anyone, especially the betrothed Cassandra Seton. He had never even thought of courting as a serious business, after a lifetime of listening to his father.

Do not involve an innocent woman in your fate, Jonathan Aubrey, he could conjure in the Earl Vane's shaky baritone.

In order to not examine that thought, he asked one of Spencer's young cousins to dance. A simple dance would be comfortable with a debutante, who would have no expectations of a man with an unmarriageable reputation and would not mind if he was desultory and preoccupied. Cassandra paired up with a man Thaxton did not recognize, one of the offensive unknown names on her card. The man looked too dandified, with a swoop of blond hair over an angelic face, and he was making her laugh.

"Thaxton," Spencer said, passing him in the dance, "why are you so tense?"

"I am not," he said, entirely aware that he was. He craned his neck as they made another pass; he saw Cassandra reach out for the man's hand in procession. She was smiling still. The irrational feeling that seized upon Thaxton would not go away—he did not want another man making her laugh. He wanted to do it.

"Thaxton," Spencer repeated, "I know this will sound impossible, but you are acting even daffier than usual."

"I know," he said flatly. "Apologies."

When the time for the second waltz arrived, Thaxton found Cassandra without delay.

"Madam?" He smiled, savoring the moment that her eyes found him, and the fact that they roamed over his form seemingly against orders from their master.

"Our dance, Lord Thaxton," she said, taking the hand that he held out. Though every facet of touching her seemed hazardous, what harm could one dance do?

When Thaxton put a hand at the small of her back and pulled her close, a total awareness of him spread over her body, with a specific fiery feeling at the crown of her head. As if every nerve in her body was energized, recognizing that what was happening now was always supposed to happen, the moment when they stood looking at each other before this waltz had always been in their future.

A rightness. It tingled.

They were far closer than was proper, held on far tighter than they should. He was so warm—dear god, did he have a fever?

"We have work to do, Cassandra," he said near her ear with a smile. Though his lips did not touch her, the sensation brought back the thrill of their kiss.

"Yes, we do," she agreed, trying to preserve the air of mystery but feeling excitement. Adventure was such a fragile thing; reality pushed on it constantly. "When should we set off?"

"From the ballroom, the séance room is one floor down and to the left. You can find your way there by yourself, correct?"

"I think."

They had begun dancing, she realized. Sometime in the course of conversation and her thoughts, he had swept her into an effortless waltz. The spinning vortex created by their feet threw the room into a blur, making the faces of the other dancers disappear. Her gown brushed his ankle as they bobbed gently, the other pairs of dancers swelling around them.

"After dinner, go downstairs," he said, his eyes traveling the room as they whirled around, as if he thought someone was listening to them. "I will leave ten minutes before you and make sure the way is clear. I am sorry you must endure any more time with Markwick."

She laughed. "I am, too."

Maybe it was the champagne, but she felt giddy and light-headed. Thaxton led them through the dance like he had invented it, but with complete obliviousness to his own grace.

"May I tell you something, Cassandra?"

She felt his voice more than she heard it.

"Yes?"

"I feel I must kiss you again. Not here, of course. I do not know when or where, but I thought you should know."

"Do you think mentioning these things will shock me? Are you being provocative for its own sake? Or do you wish to keep kisses in the forefront of my mind for some other reason?"

"Merely a fair warning. I would not want you to be too surprised."

The music drew to a close and they finished out the steps, holding on to each other well after the last violin strain. Cassandra saw Miles, and for once he was not looking at Lucy. He was glaring at them. Thaxton's gaze followed hers; he noticed it, too.

"I will be scolded," Cassandra said, finally letting go of his solid arms. "Even though he has been shameless with his admiration of Lucy."

"It is my fault," Thaxton said, shaking his head. "If you were being courted by anyone else, he would not have the same look of fury. Miles probably thinks I am taunting him."

"Good," she said, narrowing her eyes and letting a touch of bitterness seep into her voice. "He has been following Lucy around like a lost puppy." She stopped, going back over what Thaxton had just revealed, tangled in his phrasing. "Did you say you were courting me?"

"Thank you for the dance, Miss Seton," he said, bowing and raising his voice, talking more to the crowd than her. "Enjoy the rest of your evening."

She was about to press him to explain, but Lady Dorset's hand closed over her arm in an unimpeachable grip that demanded attention, pulling her to the side of the dance floor.

"Do you recall that I told you not to dally with that monster?"

"He asked me to dance. It would have been rude to refuse."

"But the waltz!" Lady Dorset exclaimed, pausing to take a steadying breath. "That waltz was beyond careless. Anyone who looked at the two of you could see."

"Could see . . . what? Dancing?"

"The viscount was whispering in your ear, Cassie, shockingly close. I heard Spencer's mother grumble about 'brash young people,' and on the way over here, I heard Lord Hartford remark about 'the Ghost's undue interest in Dorset's daughter,' so people noticed, and your father will know by week's end."

"Jonathan does not like that nickname, and it is unspeakably crass that people insist on perpetuating it."

"You should not know that," Lady Dorset said through her teeth, pulling Cassandra back toward Miles, "nor should you care. Nor should you call him Jonathan." She turned fully on Cassandra, her face crumbling from poise into anger and resentment. "Do not ruin your impending nuptials, Cassandra, or I will make sure that your life is miserable. And do not think you can simply go back and meddle at your father's house anymore. It is unseemly that you have been allowed to do so for so long."

"Viscount Thaxton is a new friend at a house party, and there is nothing improper about him. He is Miles's blood relative, for heaven's sake," Cassandra said, her arm burning from her stepmother's touch. Lady Dorset's claw sparkled with rings bought by her father, and family heirlooms that should have been Cassandra's.

"He is the son of a madman and hermit." Lady Dorset's fury began to fray the edges of her public society manner. She had made the waltz even more of a scene than it had to be. "You have no business trifling with him, even if you are only thinking of an assignation."

It always unnerved Cassandra the way that both of her parents spoke of infidelity: casually, as if it were an accepted fact. Their feelings on the sanctity of wedding vows made it impossible for her to argue that she would not marry Miles because she did not love him. She and Lady Dorset had reached Miles's side, where he entertained Lucy and a flock of tittering women.

He bowed low to Cassandra's stepmother, making too much of a show of his gratitude. His attendance to her had begun to border on groveling.

"Thank you for returning my beloved safely, Lady Dorset."

There followed an unbearable dance, in which his arms around her felt as if they were trespassing on ground already claimed by the viscount. They did not speak.

All through the everlasting dinner, she thought about the plan. She would need to get away without causing too much of a fuss. A headache usually sufficed, the tried-and-true excuse, but she found she had used that one a lot lately. Perhaps a stomach complaint? No, she did not want Eliza to think that the food had caused it. She kept an eye on Thaxton to see when he would leave and tried not to be distracted by how handsome he was, even across the room. Miles's posture was stick-straight, and he avoided looking at her too long. She could tell he wanted to question her about the viscount, but they were surrounded by dinner guests. Finally, the men left the ballroom, and the ladies adjourned to the parlor. Before she could join them, Miles emerged from the smoking room and steered her away. As they were walking, him leading her by the elbow, a man called out to Miles and urged him to hurry back to the room. Cassandra vaguely remembered his face as one of Miles's uncles when he introduced them at dinner, but she had been preoccupied in thinking about Thaxton's arms around her inside the waltz.

As soon as they were out of earshot of the crowd, Miles unloaded his ire.

"What did he say to you, the viscount?"

Cassandra stumbled a moment, ashamed that she had quite forgotten to have something at the ready should Miles ask that question.

"He said it was a wonderful party, he was so enjoying himself . . . and he congratulates you and me, bidding us a happy marriage."

"I know full well those are all things Thaxton would never say."

She could not argue with that.

"We were just chatting, Miles. I must do so at balls, you know."

"I asked that you not fraternize with him, and you blatantly disobeyed me. Do you think me a fool, that I cannot see what is going on?" He glanced around to make sure no one was paying attention to his raised voice. "I will not tolerate it, Cassandra. You will not speak to him beyond greeting, and if he asks you to dance again, your answer will be no, thank you."

"And what of Lucy?" she snapped. "Will you cease dancing with her?"

"She has nothing to do with this."

"I beg to differ."

"Leave it," he said, his words clipped and tight. "This is not a discussion for a ballroom, but I will summon you tomorrow."

"You will . . . summon me?"

"Indeed I will, as is my right."

Cassandra stayed mum, fearing that if she opened her mouth a torrent of words would come out—every miserable feeling she had about this man who had ruined her life. She would save it for when he "summoned" her, she thought, shivering with indignation.

"I will look forward to it," she said, able to measure her words but not her scorn. "I find that I have developed a headache, Miles. I think I will make my apologies to the countess and turn in early."

"See that you do," he said, his mouth turned down.

Cassandra tried to glide away gracefully, but felt more like she was stomping. The crowd in the sitting room would never demonstrate such behavior. Her stepmother did not seem to be among them. More the better if she had gone to bed early, one less explanation to make. Cassandra touched Eliza's elbow and made her good-bye, feeling a fleeting guilt at her deception.

She did not have a headache and was not going to bed. She had seen Thaxton leave ten minutes before, and it was past time to follow him. She was going to be late.

Thaxton did not think Miss Seton was coming, after all.

By five past he paced the blue parlor alone. He left the door open a crack, to signal that he was inside. He lit two candles, enough to obliterate the darkness. Music from the ball filtered down in a faint shadow of itself, leaving the ground floor of Spencer House quiet. Only one footman remained posted near the front door of the estate, in case of emergency, but he knew enough to pay no mind to Jonathan Vane wandering around at night.

Six past. He could not believe it; he had been convinced she would show.

Thaxton turned his eyes to the ceiling and sank into a chair in the corner, which emitted a cloud of dust from disuse. Foolish idea in the first place, this whole thing. He was not sure what had possessed him to invite Miss Seton to meet him alone, an act that would mean devastation to her reputation if they were caught. He drummed his fingers on a side table and resisted the urge to reach for the brandy snifter.

Eight past. Incredible.

He lifted one crystal glass, shifted it to glint off the moonlight low in the windows. It had been too long since he had enjoyed the company of a woman in the biblical sense—likely the reason behind his rash decision to extend the invitation. When things had deteriorated at home, Thaxton had found himself with a distinct lack of female companionship. Merry widows were too merry to have a fling with a man holed up in gloomy city rooms with his mad father. Debutantes were out of the question, and prostitutes . . . perish the thought.

Blast it. He was going to have a glass of brandy.

"Don't you dare," Miss Seton hissed from the doorway, wreathed in the glow of the candles. "You cannot investigate in your cups."

He sat up, putting a finger to his lips and waving her closer. Shame ruddied his cheeks in the absence of brandy to fulfill the same function. How quickly he had shot to attention. He closed the door, flicked his wrist with the precise speed required to fool the telltale creak, and turned the lock. Cassandra stared at the doorknob for a moment; he would have paid to know what she was thinking.

"Shh," he whispered. "You are late."

"I had to endure a lecture."

"About me?" he asked in an impish tone.

"Yes, about you." Her voice held something close to frustration, tempered by amusement. "We are going to have to stay apart in public, now more than ever."

"I shall have to send you notes," he said, wanting to pull her into him with the abandon of his adolescent days, before his father's approaching madness had changed his life. He resisted the whim. "I shall send you notes, and you can burn them. Fittingly covert, don't you think?"

"I am surprised how given to caprice you are, Jonathan." She smiled around the syllables of his name, and his body reacted without his consent. He slipped behind the table, which cut him off at the waist and effectively hid his tightened trousers. Her saying his name like that made him want her to whisper it, then moan it.

He cleared his throat. "I have been known to follow fancies."

"If we are to investigate," she said, "it must be . . . scientific."

"Scientific?" he repeated on a laugh. He regarded her endearingly stern expression. "We are going to investigate supernatural phenomena. Science, darling?"

"No need for pet names. I insist we approach this with the utmost skepticism."

"Easy for you to say. I assure you that if you grew up in the Vane family, you would have been taught from an early age that the afterlife exists and that it is always near."

"I think we should take a look at any family histories, while we are at it. Your father and Spencer's were very close; there must be one book on the Vane line in the library."

"You are a highly managing woman," he said, amused.

"You are an incredibly naive man," she replied, looking under the table. "There has to be a logical explanation for . . ." She waved her hands to encompass the whole of the situation. "This."

For some reason, her lack of tolerance for nonsense heartened him. He liked watching her sniff around the room, lifting knick-knacks and moving chairs. Thaxton felt that he should help, so he turned over a candlestick on the mantel and examined its bottom. Nothing of interest.

"What exactly are we looking for, Cassandra?"

"I imagine we will know it when we find it." She pointed to the corner. "Does this dumbwaiter function?"

"I believe so. Why?"

"I noticed it during the séance. Seems like a very good place to hide something, or someone."

They both crossed over to it, their paths meeting at the point of a *V*. She had brought a candle over, prepared to lean in. Thaxton unlatched the front of the small hand-pulled elevator, sliding the door open. Cassandra coughed.

"Musty," she said, the candle wavering.

"That probably means no one has opened it for some time."

"Not necessarily." She peered in, illuminating the wooden walls of the inside. "It's bigger than I thought."

"Big enough to hold the dowager countess. This parlor used to be her private room. She used the compartment to transport anything and everything, even furniture. She would sometimes climb into it to go up, instead of taking the stairs. It unnerved the newer servants."

"So it goes to the countess's chambers?"

"The portrait hall, actually. Well, the portrait hall now, though it was the old ballroom. When Spencer took over and his mother moved to the dowager estate, it was converted."

"A person hiding in here could have made the noises," she reasoned.

"But not the bell. That sound would have been muffled, and it was not—it was near the table. At the table."

"It's a start," Cassandra said, so far into the dumbwaiter that her top half had disappeared and her voice echoed.

That was when Thaxton heard the footsteps. He froze, his mind whirling—if they were found, Cassandra would be ruined. He heard the key, the little scrape into the lock. You had to wiggle it to get it to open correctly, thank goodness, because that gave him time to shove Miss Seton fully into the dumbwaiter and tumble in after her, putting his hand over her mouth to stifle her yelp.

Her eyes widened above his fingers.

"Someone's coming," he said, next to her ear. The doorknob rattled and her eyebrows arched again. He removed his hand slowly, and she took a big breath. He slid on his knees, splinters of old wood flaking off on his trousers, closed the door of the dumbwaiter, and blew out her candle. Cassandra and he were thrown into complete darkness.

He fumbled for her hand. He could hear her shallow breathing, too fast, panicked. The key clicked into position, and the lock opened.

"I told you," Spencer's voice boomed. "They would not be so *idiotic*, Eliza. I am sure Thaxton and Miss Seton have gone to bed."

Thaxton could tell that Spencer knew they were there. His tone bore both smile and reprimand.

Eliza's heels clicked across the room; he could hear her run a hand over the drapery. "I highly doubt that. But they are not here."

"Then they are clever enough to evade us—leave them alone."

"Percival," Eliza said, perilously close to the dumbwaiter, "I have half a mind to think you are encouraging them."

"I am not encouraging her—Thaxton is notoriously hard to deal with; he is not a good catch. But him, yes. Miss Seton is quite literally the best he could do for himself."

The temperature in the dumbwaiter had risen with the door closed. It would not have bothered Thaxton under normal circumstances, but Cassandra's hand softened under his, and she smelled enchanting. The space might have fit one person, but with two it was cramped. Yet being this close to Cassandra was in no way uncomfortable. When he warned her that he was going to kiss her again, he hadn't meant for it to be so soon. He had wanted to drag it out, make her wonder, make her a bit crazy.

But he was doing it nonetheless, quite before he could stop himself.

She gasped when his mouth found hers in the darkness, a little sound that dissolved into him and fueled his ardor. He caressed her cheek, but he could not see it. She tensed for a moment, her fingers sliding under the lapel of his jacket. The way her lips moved, he could tell she wanted to speak. He kissed her nose, her temple, her eyes. Eliza was speaking, farther away from them.

"I cannot argue with that. Either way, we must get back to the ball before we are missed. I imagine the dowager countess . . ."

Her voice receded, and the door clicked shut. Thaxton had his nose pressed on Cassandra's cheek, unmoving.

"They were talking about us," he said.

"And no wonder, Jonathan. Are you going to move?"

He shook his head against her face.

"No."

❧

Unbelievable. Thaxton's nose nuzzled her once more before he pulled her closer to him, continuing the kiss. His arm belted her waist; his other hand braced against the floor behind her. These kisses had no urgency; his pace spoke of time to explore without fear of discovery. They wandered down her neck, perilously close to her décolletage. She inhaled, her chest rising, and arched into him. Her hand found the back of his head, fingers weaving into the freshly shorn hair.

Her gown billowed out behind him, seeming to engulf him in taffeta. Her eyes could not adjust to the enclosed space, so she could not anticipate where he would touch her next. He pulled her closer, returning to her mouth. He traced her lips with the tip of his tongue.

"Oh," she heard a voice say. Hers? Yes, hers.

"Mmm." And that was Thaxton's.

First his tongue, then his teeth, grazing her bottom lip, turning the kiss from something conventional to something wild. Her hands nudged under his jacket, tracing his waistcoat, feeling his chest underneath. He made a noise, a growl of assent, and deepened the kiss again, coaxing her tongue out.

Then he broke the embrace abruptly. His hand rested on her breast, but it had stopped moving. Until that moment, she had not realized just how far they had gone over acceptable lines. Her flesh felt somehow lighter in his hand, and her nipple had gone harder than it did on very cold days.

"Jonathan?" she asked into the darkness. "Is something wrong?"

As soon as she voiced it, Cassandra realized that something was very wrong. In the course of their embrace, they had wedged into the corner of the dumbwaiter. He had virtually crawled on top of her. She was pinned, unable to move the wall of Thaxton.

"Yes. No," he said. She felt him shake his head, and his hand dropped to her lap. "I am not sure." He rested his chin on her shoulder and inhaled slowly. "Do you smell that?"

"My perfume?" she said, not sure if she should be offended. From his tone, it sounded as if he didn't like what was in his nostrils. "Me?"

"No, darling. Not you. I know what you smell like—I would never mistake it." He shifted, turning her around so they were both facing the wall. "That—does not smell like you. It smells cloying and sickly sweet. It is not you, it is not me, so . . ."

"Someone was in here," she said, catching the scent. "Recently." Her hand searched in the darkness until she hit on something—a scrap of fabric, smelling strongly of whatever perfumes the wearer had doused herself in. It had been caught on a protruding nail; it was a lucky thing that neither of them had hurt themselves.

"Scientific enough for you?" he teased, placing one more kiss on her neck before sliding over to the door. He opened the elevator slowly, the luminosity of the candles expanding into the darkness. The light felt raw.

"Come now," he said, scooting out and offering his hand to her. "It is a bit . . . overheated in there."

She landed in his arms, both of them covered in a thin layer of dust. His hair was slightly frosted over with it. Cassandra fought the urge to make him define what had just happened, what the devil was going on between them.

"Signs point to an accomplice," she said instead. "Though we have no conclusive proof."

"I am having trouble thinking," he answered, running a hand through her hair, his fingers brushing her scalp. The way he looked at her, eyes squinted and intense, made her feel vastly uneasy.

She wanted to say, *Why are you acting like this? What are we doing? What does this mean?*

Instead she said, "We can theorize that someone was in the dumbwaiter. It merits further investigation."

"Oh, indeed," he said, arching a brow. His hands were on her waist, both familiar and encroaching at the same time. "Exhaustive reconnaissance. Proper spying."

"The music has stopped," she said, bereft of any wit.

"The ball is probably over," he said. "We can sneak back to our rooms soon. But not quite yet."

Inconvenient, because she had the mighty urge to flee. He had not released her, though it was far past time to do so. She shifted, and he tightened his arms.

"Stop that," he said.

"What?"

"Do not feel badly about that kiss."

Every reply to that statement created something she could not voice. She was seized with a terror that he would kiss her again—and they could not go on like that. It would be too easy for her to fall for him . . . he made her sensibilities take leave entirely. What had started out as a harmless flirtation had become a dodgy tryst.

"All right, then," he said. He let go of her, seeming to sense the change in her demeanor. He sank into one of the chairs, lounging indolently. "Since this is your investigation, what is the next step?"

"Oh. I had not thought of it."

"I think we need to inspect Lucy's chambers. See if there is any evidence of foul play."

"One might think you are beginning to disbelieve her powers." She smiled.

"It does not matter, Cassandra," he said, "but it is diverting for now. Even if Lucy is a complete put-on, my family is cursed, and I am"—he gestured theatrically in the candlelight, mocking himself—"the ill-fated thirteenth earl."

"Hogwash."

He folded his hands and straightened his back, turned a bit steely. His lips, previously so mobile in their kiss, drew into a grim line.

"As you say. It is a simple fact of my life, no matter what you believe."

"It is not a fact, my lord, it is an assumption. Now, you said we should search Lucy's room." Cassandra tapped her foot, thinking. She needed to keep Thaxton on track or he would grow maudlin—she was beginning to get the ebb and tide of his moods. If one could engage him, he would not slip back into the wild fantasies of the nightmare his father had imposed on him.

"I imagine we will need a key," he said.

"I know where Eliza keeps the master key for the guest chambers."

"Stealing. You minx."

"Borrowing. I will beg sickness at dinner tomorrow," she said, the plan solidifying in her head, "and you will make sure that Lucy stays entertained."

"I cannot promise entertainment, but I can find some way to hold her attention. Even if it means annoying her to her very last nerve."

"Good. Stall as long as you can."

"And you will rifle through her drawers?"

"I suppose. Do you have a better idea?"

"Sod the whole thing and kiss me again?"

"Jonathan, honestly."

Her attempt at exasperation was no match for his charm, creating a space devoid of words. It pulsed until he spoke again.

"You should go," he said, consulting his pocket watch with an exaggerated casualness. "Now that we have a plan for tomorrow, you should be safe in your room in case that rat Miles sniffs around to say good night."

"Heaven forfend."

"I shudder to think of it." He stood, kissing her cheek as if it were merely chaste affection. "Send word tomorrow after you complete the mission. Good night, Miss Seton."

She managed a curtsy that felt strange once she did it, mumbled a good-bye, and made haste from the room. She did not let out a breath until she began to ascend the stairs. She was having second thoughts about having engaged in this game at all (third, fourth, fifth thoughts, were she honest). Thaxton was a man who needed plenty of help, but she was not the one to give it to him. She could not make it a cause to fix his life. As it stood, she was already nearly half in love with him.

One of the maids must have lit the hearth in her room; it glowed cozy and orange. No sign of Miles. A note from Eliza lay on the desk:

*I stopped to see if you were feeling better. I was here
at 11. Curious that you were not.*
—E.

Cassandra was going to have a lot of explaining to do the next day. It
was time to tell Eliza that—tell her what, exactly? That Thaxton had
kissed her, repeatedly, many different places, that he had rumpled her
gown and absolutely destroyed her coif? That he was not forthcoming
about his intentions, that he seemed comfortable letting this situation
progress unhindered? That he claimed he could never marry but acted
as if he was pursuing her?

She flopped onto the bed, engulfed in pillows, and her corset
tugged at her ribs. It was far too late to wake anyone for help, so she
was going to have to undress herself, not a savory prospect. A half hour
of bending, tilting, and shimmying later, she was wrested from the
architecture of the dress. Her nightgown had never felt so freeing, and
she had never felt so exhausted.

Fate was merciful, and she slept through the night.

Fate did not hold up, however, because Lady Dorset requested her
presence early in the morning. Cassandra waited in the little sitting
room of her stepmother's suite, fidgeting. She could only guess at what
the marchioness might have to say, but it was certainly nothing good.
All she could think about was Thaxton and their plan.

She stood when the door opened, held for Lady Dorset.

"Good morning, Cassandra. I trust sleep has knocked the silly
notions out of your head."

"Respectfully, my lady, I have done nothing wrong."

Her stepmother's chin rose. "Excusing yourself after dinner last
night, after that wicked waltz. Hardly befitting a lady of your stature or
complimentary to dear Mr. Markwick."

"I do not want to marry Miles."

It was out before she could stop it, but there it was.

"You know your marriage contract was signed well before I became marchioness. Your father needs those coalfields. And he was wise to arrange it—your unmarried life is carried by the money he made. Cassandra, I shall be straightforward. I merely want you out of my way."

"Miles does not want to marry me either," Cassandra said, wishing it wasn't a plea. "He only needs my dowry to save his estate, since the loss of those same coalfields bankrupted his family. If they would have kept them, I would not be in this position."

"It is useless for you to wish things had been different. However, if you continue to consort with Thaxton, I will not hesitate to write to your father."

"Lady Dorset, please. I promise I will concentrate on Miles. Just do not write to my father—please let me sort this out myself."

Lady Dorset studied her for a long moment, with no indication of what she was thinking and not a trace of sympathy to her cause.

"I would rather not leave," she said finally. "I am enjoying the company, and this Lucy Macallister is a most interesting addition to the party. But understand that if you step another toe out of line, I will not even write Lord Dorset. I will intervene and take both you and Miles back to our estate."

"I understand," Cassandra said, grateful, allowing it to show in her voice. "My thanks to you."

"Go," Lady Dorset snapped.

Cassandra dropped a rushed curtsy and fled.

Chapter Six

"Things have gone too far," Thaxton told Spencer, having convinced him that an afternoon of solitude in the library would be just the thing. It had not taken much persuading: Spencer's pride and joy, the billiards table, also resided in the library.

"I suspected as much," he said, crouching to line up a shot, his eye following the trajectory.

The whole thing called for a glass of scotch, a very hard-earned single drink. Thaxton leaned on his cue like a walking stick, his other hand on the glass. He was eating more regularly, and his veins did not feel like they were drying up, absorbing the alcohol and withering. He had become off-balance, he was realizing. What he had been doing to himself had made everything worse.

It was his turn, and there was not a shot on the table. He looked it over; he had nothing, no options. Like every day of his life, spread out before him.

"All infernal angles." Spencer shook his head. "Sorry, chap."

Thaxton hit the cue ball, not aiming.

"She cannot marry him," he said, without qualifying the pronouns.

"She can," Spencer said, picking up the shot that Thaxton had unwittingly set up for him. "She could, I mean."

"It would be a tragedy. A waste. There must be someone else. What do you know of Amberson? Baronet, pleasant enough? If not him, there must be a stray American businessman around here."

"Your solution is to play matchmaker? Why not marry her yourself? Ah, but I forgot your obsession with superstitious drivel." Spencer gestured with his billiard stick. "Take your shot."

There was one this time—an easy line into a side pocket. The click of the billiard balls, the heavy thud into the pocket, the smooth baize of the table: it was all somewhat reassuring. Physics worked, gravity prevailed. Miss Seton's existence changed things, but the world still worked according to natural law.

Thaxton lost two games to Spencer before they parted to change for dinner. He did not feel bad about the defeat; he was far too unfocused for that. He was mainly ruminating on the institution of marriage, something that he had not given much thought to before. He could see the advantages. Spencer's own relationship was a model of an equal match. He and the countess supported each other and seemed to make the other better.

Thaxton had never considered himself anything but alone.

Solo, *unus*, solitary, however you wanted to phrase it, he thought as he dressed. He was an island. Or a dead end. He would not be continuing his family line, so no wife was required or expected of him. His father had put it thusly: "Do not bother falling in love, my son."

Sound advice.

By the time Thaxton reached the parlor outside the dining room, it was full to bursting. He scanned the room for Miles and Lucy—in a corner—but he did not approach them immediately. He watched them for a while, engaged in conversation. They did not seem to be affected by Cassandra's absence, though he was sure that Miles had been told of her "illness." He did not look like a man concerned about his fiancée's well-being. Thaxton felt a surge of envy mixed with resentment; had he been in Markwick's position, he would have been at Cassandra's bedside, not hovering over some other woman.

The dinner procession began. Miles and Lucy lined up behind him, which was inconvenient for the moment, as far as keeping an eye on them. But it meant that they would be directly across the table, so he could dominate Lucy's attention with ceaseless questions about her work in Spiritualism.

Spencer and Eliza sat at the head of the table, forced by decorum and the dowager to bow to tradition. Thaxton should be attending them as well, but Spencer had been kind enough to honor his request for seating near Miles. He had not even asked for an explanation.

"Good evening, Thaxton," Miles said as he sat down, the words forced from between his thin little lips. And his small teeth, Thaxton noted, his terribly small weasel teeth. It was not the first time he fantasized about knocking them out of his cousin's face.

"And to you, Markwick. Where is your lovely fiancée?"

The question earned a glare.

"Cassandra is ill, unfortunately. She sends her regrets. We spent the afternoon together . . . she seems pale." Miles's smile curled in mockery. "If she does not recover soon, I think it best for me to take her back home to prepare for our wedding."

Thaxton had a few answers spring to mind, first and foremost being *She doesn't love you.* But Miles did not seem to care that this was the case; he seemed indifferent to Cassandra, which made Thaxton angrier. He opted not to answer at all, but to imagine grabbing the villain by the lapels and shaking him until his meager brain fell out of his skull.

"Have you set a date?" Lucy asked, with a forced nonchalance that gave her away.

"Three weeks from tomorrow," Miles said with exactly the same passion one would give to a doctor's visit. "Her parents have sent word that everything is well begun."

Thaxton recognized his own expression in Lucy's face. They both could not hide their revulsion at the thought of this union, the utter disbelief that the participants were going forward as planned. As if something were truly, deeply wrong with a universe in which this could happen. He felt a twinge of camaraderie, a decidedly atypical feeling to have about a woman who had told him to die.

"Miss Mac—pardon, Lucy," he said, "what will you do after your holiday at Spencer House? Will you go back to Scotland?"

She appeared startled that he was being nice to her.

"I came here initially by invite of the London Spiritualist Society. You may have heard of them—the group has become popular among wealthy ladies, though I think they look upon us as a novelty. The aim of the society is to demonstrate and teach the healing power of Spiritualist practice."

Thaxton held in his contempt. Healing? From what he had seen of Lucy's mediumship, it did not convey healthfulness. The séance had made him feel more divided, farther away from the rest of his fellow humans. With the possible exception of Miss Seton.

He noticed Lucy frown slightly at his prolonged silence. Time for a pleasantry.

"How nice," Thaxton said.

"It is," Lucy said, smiling. "They have asked me to consider staying permanently." Her eyes flicked to Miles. "I have not made a decision yet."

"London has its advantages," Thaxton said. As long as Lucy kept talking, there was no chance she was anywhere near her room. If he needed to spout nonsense to buy Cassandra time, he would. "But I imagine Scotland does as well. I have never been there myself. Your whole family is there, yes?"

"Oh, aye," she said. "Miles can tell you. He spent a good deal of time with my father, learning to manage a small estate."

"Really now?" Thaxton's gaze drifted to Miles. "How industrious of you, Markwick. I thought you said you could not find an occupation."

Lady Beatrice, who was seated at their table, perked up. Thaxton realized there must have been an arch in his voice, the whiff of gossip, if it interested that lady.

"Not a proper one. But now that I have inherited my father's estate—my future wife and I—it would behoove me to be prepared for that, Thaxton. The old manor needs significant repairs."

"And, of course, Cassandra's dowry will more than support the financial stability of such an endeavor." *Good lord,* Thaxton thought as soon as he closed his mouth, *I sound angry.*

"I would appreciate it if you did not refer to my fiancée in such a familiar manner," Miles said evenly. "I am sure she did not give you permission to do so."

Lucy laughed lightly. It looked as if she had prodded Miles in the ribs, but it was not a big enough movement for the table to notice.

"You English. So stuffy."

As the first course was served, everyone's attention turned to the ritual of eating. Soft murmurs surrounded them. Thaxton willed the minutes by, hoping Cassandra wasn't dawdling.

Lady Beatrice Valentine talked about a great many things; she could always be counted on when no one else felt like talking. Lucy was trapped, as she would never dare leave when a lady was holding forth, so Thaxton's job of distraction became easy. He watched the scene and felt mild annoyance at the way Miles chewed.

How long, conceivably, could it take to inspect a bedroom? Thaxton could hear his heart pounding with the endless ticking of the clock. The last plates were being cleared and people were adjourning either to the parlor or to chambers. The whole process had taken more than two hours, and Lucy was back to chatting with Miles before they parted ways.

Thaxton excused himself to Spencer and did not join the men for drinks. He got away with a fleeting look of wariness from the earl. Thaxton had an inkling he was going to be confronted about his intentions toward Miss Seton soon, and he had no idea what he would say. He did not even have an idea what the rest of the evening held.

He found his answer when he got to his room and found a note, unsigned, waiting on his desk.

Need to talk. Labyrinth L, R, R, L, L.

෴

How to conduct an illicit search of a rival's room was not something taught to young girls at Cheltenham Ladies' College, so Cassandra had devised her own plan. She retrieved the master key from its case in the head butler's room, after having him called to the ballroom on a wild-goose chase for a lady's bonnet that did not exist. She crept up the stairs with the key in a secret pocket she had sewn into her skirt. Cheltenham had provided a few fortunate skills, at least.

Dinnertime meant that the hallways of the guests' bedrooms were deserted. Lucy's room sat at the end of the hall on the third floor, she having been a late addition with no rank to speak of. She was in a small wing with the only other rooms around her being storage space. Though all was quiet, Cassandra's heart hammered as she turned the key. A little click and the door creaked open.

Lucy's small hearth burned low, which meant that eventually some-one would be along to check it, so time was limited. The room did not look too much different from the other guest rooms, but the woman's occupation filled it with a unique air. Lucy's séance kimono lay draped on the reading chair, managing to look more elegant and mysterious than any of Cassandra's gowns.

A stack of pamphlets lay on the bedside table. She rifled through them carefully: *The Spiritualist, The Medium and Daybreak, A Treatise on Manifestations of Ectoplasmic Material in Controlled Séance Settings.*

So, she was serious, then, at least about her studies. Spiritualism was not something she was playing at.

The vanity's surface teemed with little tubes and pots that Cassandra did not recognize. She opened one—rouge or lip stain. Darker than the second marchioness would have ever allowed. She had the distinct urge to try it on, but there was no time for dress up.

She opened a drawer, feeling invasive. Surely this was not right, but after the events of the past few days, she did not see any way of learning more about the medium. The breakfast talk had been full of platitudes and designed to entertain the ladies, but it told Cassandra nothing of Lucy's real feelings. If only she could have a plain conversation with Lucy, to find some common ground and settle the matter of Miles. Cassandra did not want him, and she was the reason Lucy and he could not pursue their obvious interest.

The drawer held a riot of stockings and undergarments: Lucy Macallister was not a neat woman. Nothing was folded, though some of the stockings stayed rolled into little balls. Cassandra gingerly began searching; she wanted to make sure it was not obvious that anything had been disturbed. There was a small box, wooden and thick, carved with the moon and stars. She fumbled around on the side of the heavy box, finding an expensive silver latch that easily popped open. Inside, lying on the golden silk lining, was a pack of elaborately drawn cards, esoteric. The Magician, a wizened man atop a globe, holding aloft a scepter that gleamed to the borders of the card. A knight with swords sticking in the ground around him, as if they hemmed him in, The Five of Swords. Temperance, an angel with feminine features, head down as in contemplation. They looked like they might be used for divination. Cassandra lost about five minutes before she remembered she was supposed to be investigating, not entranced by art.

She put the packet back where it had been.

Next to it, her fingers hit upon something hard. She slowly pulled the obstacle out—a pair of leather straps with small wooden blocks attached to each. The contraptions had buckles and looked as if they had been made out of whatever was at hand, not purchased. Experimentally, Cassandra knocked the blocks together. Voilà, rapping ghost.

Fraud.

Later, she wished she had stopped there. But she just had to open the lid of the jewelry box. She had to see what Lucy Macallister considered precious.

❧❧❧

Cassandra paced the dead end of the labyrinth, worrying that she had given Thaxton the wrong directions. She retraced her path, only to find it correct. She retraced it again, correct again. Her anxiety had reached a fever pitch by the time night had fallen, especially when a servant had nearly caught her in Lucy's room.

It had been worth it, though. She had not one, but two very interesting things to share with the viscount.

Her day had contained a series of homilies about him. Lady Dorset preached that Thaxton was poisonous. She maintained it was not wise to "play this game with him," as she put it. Thankfully, the marchioness did not quite know the extent of the game. And then, of course, the summons from Miles at lunch. She met him in the library, and he had said, in no uncertain terms, that they would be married in three weeks. He mentioned that her father would have been disappointed if he had seen her behavior at the ball, chastising her as if he were a parent himself. He said he hoped that there would not be another performance like that; he implied it would be easier if she demurely accepted her fate. He more than implied she should never again so much as look at Jonathan Vane. He expressly ordered it, this time with a veiled threat to drag her out of the house party, echoing the words of Lady Dorset.

The tension between them made it even easier to beg off dinner due to sickness, especially since he could not accuse her of being with Thaxton, since the viscount held his stalwart position at the table. She did not think Miles wanted to see her any more than she wanted to see him.

Now she heard footsteps approaching and shrank back into the shadows in case it was a stray party guest. Thaxton rounded the corner, the moonlight making him a sleek silhouette.

"There you are," he said, drawing her into his arms as soon as he saw her. She gave a little gasp, not of offense, but of surprise and delight. "There was a faulty part of our plan, you know."

"Oh, no," she said, shaken by his statement as much as by the fact that she relaxed into his arms without much prompting.

"Just that a night without you was torture."

"Goodness, Jonathan. Be serious."

"I am serious. The dinner table without you was the eighth circle of hell."

"Not the ninth?"

"Lucy, false prophet; Miles, panderer; I, seducer. Eighth."

"Seducer?"

"If you would give me the chance. But your note seemed urgent. What have you found?"

"These."

Cassandra extracted herself from his arms and went to retrieve the evidence. She held up the strange contraptions she'd found in Lucy's stocking drawer, shoved into the back corner. When the blocks struck each other, they produced a very distinct sound. She clapped them together, raising an exultant eyebrow at Thaxton.

"Recognize that?" she said.

"Sounds like our talkative ghost. Ingenious." He took them, turning them over in his hands, unbuckling one of them. "Worn, I suppose?"

"Under the skirts, I think."

She very much expected him to make an off-color joke, but he remained silent. He stared at the proof—she could not read his expression.

"I half hoped you would not find anything," he said. "Part of me wanted to believe the séance was confirmation of my unalterable fate."

"There is a freedom to believing in fate, I imagine. Less responsibility for your actions." She paused. "But I think this means both the wailing woman and the séance can be somehow explained, that they are the same issue."

Yet on the question of unalterable fate, she thought, rolling the second artifact she found in Lucy's room around in her palm. She was no longer sure that she should even mention that she had also found a pair of Miles's cuff links with Lucy's jewelry. The engraving on both little studs a damning *MRM*. Cassandra did not know Miles's middle name, but it was clear enough who owned them. What did it matter to Thaxton that on top of Lucy being a fraud, she was also Miles's mistress?

Neither was it necessary to tell him that though she had been joking before, she was now seriously considering running away. Considering how much she would need to support herself, likely places that would take in a woman without asking too much about her previous life.

"What else?" Thaxton said. He was looking at her with narrowed eyes, with obvious suspicion. "There is something else."

She nearly burst into tears. He knew she was upset, *that* he noticed. She steeled herself.

"It is irrelevant to the investigation," she said.

"Cassandra. What is it?"

She did not answer him, but opened her palm. He held one of the cuff links up to the sky; the silver glinted and the initials came into view as he rotated it.

"What I am about to say is only half-serious," he growled, "but if you want me to kill him, I will."

"Were it that easy," she lamented.

"Do not marry him," he said, the words spilling out as if they were pursued.

"I do not have much of a choice," she said, sounding much more stoic than she felt. No matter how much she enjoyed the viscount's company, he was not going to save her from anything in the state he was in. "In any case, it is not your concern. With the discovery of those wooden blocks, I think we can safely say Lucy Macallister has no supernatural powers."

"But what of the bell?"

"I assume she had some other trick. No matter how mad your father is, Thaxton, that woman was lying to get a rise out of you. Why—that is what we do not know."

"Lucy and I had never met before this week. Why me, even if she is connected to Miles? Why bother?"

"Your history with Miles, the rivalry?"

"There is no rivalry, at least on my part—he is beneath my notice most of the time. I endeavor to ignore him, not goad him. Does this not seem like an elaborate and hurtful prank, if it was just to scare me? I am already an exile. Miles is reentering society. What does it matter? It seems like a lot of effort to put forth."

"It cannot have been just to scare you," she said, peering up at the sky through the top of the labyrinth. It was a cool night, one that would be outright cold in a few hours. But that was not what made her shiver. "They want something from you."

"But what? And what do we do?" he asked, sounding as if he truly had no idea how to proceed. The truth was, neither did she. Until his father wrote back, they would not know if Lucy had been to London.

"Wait. See if your father writes back, see if they try to pull any other capers." The moon was climbing higher. "We should get back to our rooms. Miles may try to check on me."

Cassandra watched Thaxton's face tighten.

"Do not let him touch you," he said, prowling toward her. "Cassandra. Do not marry him. It enrages me that he even shares air with you."

"I do not intend to," she replied, trying to maintain her equilibrium. He stepped in front of her again so fast that her vision swam. She raised a hand against his chest, stopping his offensive. "Not that it is any of your business."

"Ah," he said, recoiling from her gesture. "There it is."

"Hmm?"

"I knew after what happened in the dumbwaiter that it was a matter of time before you told me I was a blackguard. I cannot help it . . . I want to kiss you."

"I grant that it was an enjoyable diversion, but we cannot go on."

"Why?"

Not a whine, not a plea, just a bald question. And she could not think of a proper answer.

"It is . . . unwise."

"I am a gentleman—mad or not—and if you think what we have been doing is untoward, it will cease. I thought—I rather thought we were both having fun."

"Yes," she said. "Too much."

"But what of the investigation?"

"I do not know why you would need me from here," she said, though she very much wanted him to need her, "but the house party will go on as planned, and if you require help, I am a note away."

"I see," he said. "Farewell, then, Miss Seton. A thank-you is in order, I believe."

"Not at all, we both . . ."

"Thank you, nonetheless. Good night."

The viscount turned back to navigate out of the labyrinth, and Cassandra was left to ponder the implications of that curt *I see*.

❧❦☙

So, he had gotten roaring drunk. He got properly shot in the neck, he hit the benzine, he got corned, however you wanted to term it. He did so because he thought he might love the girl.

That would not do.

It would not do especially because she had all but told him it was over between them by calling off the investigation. So, if he loved her, it opened up a new world of torture. He would have to watch her marry another man (not Miles, if fate was kind) and then inevitably run into her at parties, where they would make strained conversation. She would grow increasingly uneasy around him, and he would never be able to erase the memory of their strange passion.

Eventually, he assumed, she would stop going out of her way to greet him. The thought festered like a canker.

Thaxton fell asleep in front of the hearth, leaning back against a chair, sprawled on the floor. It was how Sutton found him the next morning. The viscount opened his eyes to the valet looming over him, a look of panic on his usually unsympathetic face.

"Kind of you to fret, Sutton, but I am not dead. Mostly not dead."

"Yes, I see, my lord. It is a relief." He wrung his hands a few times over. "But there is something . . ."

Thaxton felt his stomach drop, not the most pleasant feeling when one has been hitting a bottle. Sutton had left his sentence dangling like a sail in choppy wind.

"For god's sake, man, what is it?"

"Your door, my lord."

"What of it?"

"There is—there seems to be a marking on it."

"Cannot rule out the possibility," he said, pulling himself up to the sofa, "that I crashed into it last night, scuffed it with my boot or dented an old slat."

"No, my lord, not like that. It is . . . we think it is blood."

"Are you quite serious?" Thaxton rubbed his bleary eyes and crossed over to his desk. Maybe he was still soused. He could have sworn Sutton said his door was covered with blood.

"Nan—the head maid, my lord—says it is, and she saw enough of it while Spencer was growing up, terrorizing the household. She knows what blood looks like."

Thaxton regarded the back of the door, which looked ordinary enough.

"Blood as if someone had hurt themselves?" He looked down at his scruffy attire, slept in and crinkled, but not stained. "I realize I was foxed, but I do not think I harmed myself."

"You do not understand, Lord Thaxton," Sutton said, a faint thread of exasperation running under his dismay. "There is a symbol on your door, drawn in blood."

"Oh?" he said, throwing back the remains of the whisky in his glass, stale from the night before. Thaxton assumed at this point that he was hallucinating, the first steps of descending into madness, and he decided to embrace it. There was blood on his door, a symbol. All right, then.

"Sir?" Sutton asked, flummoxed.

"You should tell Spencer, I suppose. Have it cleaned up."

Sutton's reply was lost to the spectacle of Miss Seton, throwing the door open and tearing into the room past the traumatized valet. She stood just past the threshold, her eyes scanning the room frantically until she saw him.

"Jonathan," she breathed with visible relief. "Oh, thank goodness."

Reflexively, he tried to pat his hair down, as it stood up in random chunks. With his hand halfway to his head, he realized that he had no reason to impress her anymore.

"Eliza told me about your door—she is trying to control the talk around the estate. I panicked, I admit. I thought something might have happened to you. Of course, the servants mostly already know—"

"I'm sorry, Miss Seton," he said, carefully formal, "but I have no idea what you are ranting about. And you cannot be here."

She turned to her side, where the face of the door loomed. He caught a peripheral glimpse of angry red slashes, but her frantic mood took his attention first. Cassandra was behaving as if a life, his life, was in danger.

She gestured grandly—of course she did, her damned always-mobile hands—and went so far as to stamp her foot.

"Have you not seen this?" She pointed.

"I had not bothered," he said, sinking into his desk chair, bringing himself nearer to the whisky. If also nearer to his scandalized valet. "Is it horrifying?"

Thaxton knew Sutton was dying to say something about the unaccompanied banshee in the door of the bachelor's quarters.

"Look," she said angrily. She ran her finger through the drawing on the door, and it came away dripping with a rapidly browning red. "Look, Jonathan."

He finally did. There was indeed a giant symbol on his door. It almost looked like a letter *t*, yet much longer on the stem with a bowed horizontal line—meaningless, and therefore it looked esoteric, but he would recognize it anywhere. Scrawled through all of his father's notebooks. It was most assuredly drawn in blood.

Thaxton had risen to his feet before he knew it.

"Get Spencer," he said to Sutton, hearing his voice as if from a distance. "I need you to get Spencer."

The valet slunk out of the room, after one more glare at Miss Seton, who was not budging.

"What is it? You know what it is," she said.

"Not exactly," he said, turning back to his hearth, not wanting to look at the door or her. "But since I did not send a note for you, I am not in need of your services."

"Are you . . . are you pouting at me, Thaxton?"

"Not at you. Away from you."

"Oh, my goodness," she said, sounding stupefied over his shoulder. "You are angry with me."

"I am not angry," he said, tilting his head back a bit so that she could view the offensive pout. "I am disappointed."

"As am I. But setting aside our thwarted affair, a symbol drawn on your door in blood is a threat. It is not a joke. It is not a harmless hoax like the séance. And I will not allow you to go all drunken and dissolute when you are this vulnerable."

He laughed darkly.

"You will not allow me?" He poured a generous two fingers of whisky into the glass, swirling the liquid around as he sat back down. "You bloody well can't stop me."

If he had not felt so desolate, Thaxton might have enjoyed the way Cassandra took on the air of a bull about to stampede. She was about to unleash a speech on him; he could see it in the way her lips pursed, the way she tensed. Fortunately, Spencer spared him by stalking in, Eliza behind him.

"When did you wake up?" he asked briskly. "Sutton was to tell me the moment he roused you. And good lord, Miss Seton, you should *not* be in here."

"I have not been awake more than ten minutes," Thaxton said, sounding far calmer than he felt. "And as for Miss Seton, I told her the same thing."

"It is a moot point," she said.

"You are certain you are not hurt?" Spencer asked Thaxton.

"I am intact," he answered. "That symbol is from my father's notebooks, so supernatural or not, I feel I should go home."

Spencer shook his head in the negative.

"I cannot allow that."

"Your father's notebooks?" asked Cassandra, unable to leave well enough alone.

Beside him, Eliza had bent down, peering at the carpet. "Has anyone seen there is blood on the floor? There is a trail . . ."

Cassandra looked down. "All the way to the balcony."

No one rushed to follow it, but everyone crept forward. Before they reached the balcony, Thaxton halted. He saw the blood trailing out and put his arm up to block Miss Seton's path.

"The women should not go out there," he said.

Eliza scoffed but did not go any farther.

"He is right, darling," Spencer said. "We have no idea what is out there."

Thaxton was amazed when he did not hear an argument from Cassandra, but knew better than to look back at her. That was how people turned to pillars of salt. He pulled aside the curtain, Spencer behind him. The latch on the door was heavy, but it was not locked.

"I never opened that, Spence," he said quietly. "Someone has been here."

As they opened the door, Thaxton could feel Miss Seton on her toes behind him, straining to see without moving forward. Glancing to Spencer, he saw that he was fixated on a spot at the edge of the balcony, where there was a pool of black. He slunk closer while Spencer stayed behind.

"My god," he said, realizing what it was.

❧

"Get back," Spencer said, whirling around to them, closing the balcony door on Thaxton and pushing Eliza and Cassandra into the room.

"What is it?" Cassandra demanded. "The shape in the corner of the balcony?"

"A raven," he said, glancing behind him. "A dead raven."

Eliza looked confused. "Thaxton killed a raven?"

"No," Spencer and Cassandra said at the same time, albeit with very different inflections.

"He did not do this," she added. "He is not mad. He is miserable."

"Correct," Spencer said.

"You left him out there with a dead bird," Eliza said. "Who is to say he is not painting his face for war and screaming to the sky?"

"He is vomiting, actually," Spencer said.

"He is not mad, Eliza," Cassandra insisted.

"Oh, good," Eliza said, throwing up her hands. "Tell him to aim away from my hydrangeas."

Cassandra tried to see Thaxton through the window, but he must have been too far into the corner of the balcony. The worry she felt had ramped up, threatening to boil over. She had to tell Eliza and Spencer what had been going on—or a version of it.

Thaxton came back in, closing the balcony door, his head down and shoulders slumped. He looked gray.

"Should I get a doctor?" Spencer asked.

He shook his head. "No, no. No need."

Cassandra fought the urge to press the issue; someone should look at him, to be sure. He was not in the best of health overall, and the current predicament was not helping.

"I feel it is time that we admit this is not a ghost," Spencer said, with a quick glance at his wife. "And find out why someone is targeting Thax."

Cassandra's eyes shot to the viscount's at the same time his met hers.

"We—Lord Thaxton and I—have our guesses," she said.

"Miss Seton has a guess. I do not care," Thaxton amended. "Might I add that you can do nothing to keep me here, should I choose to leave? Spencer. I am a grown man."

"*You*," Spencer said, "are not in your right mind."

Cassandra watched Thaxton hear those words, watched his body go strained.

"Of course not. That is what everyone says—I am insane, correct? The last scion of a tragic family, slowly cracking? Fine. Allow me to lose my mind safely at home."

Spencer ignored him and nodded his head at Cassandra. "You have a guess, Miss Seton?"

Cassandra looked to the viscount again, but he was looking away resolutely. She had no idea how much to reveal, where to even begin.

"We have been investigating," Thaxton said before she could open her mouth. "Investigating the séance. Miss Seton suspects Lucy Macallister."

"You have been what?" Eliza said, an indictment.

"I thought it was phony," Cassandra said, "at least that was how it began. At this point, I think that Lucy Macallister is actively trying to convince Thaxton he is mad."

"Why would she want to do that?" Eliza asked.

"I have no idea. But I do know that the whole séance was fabricated, and I have proof. If anyone should be leaving this house, it is she."

"Enough for now," Spencer said definitively. "We will have the bird cleaned up, as well as Lord Thaxton. Pray that gossip does not spread, and we will discuss this further when the rest of the party is otherwise engaged. The house is stirring."

Cassandra tried to catch Thaxton's eye while Eliza shuttled her out of the room, but he had crossed his arms and turned toward the balcony.

"Do not let him leave," Spencer said to Sutton.

Eliza shut the door behind them, and Cassandra found herself facing the formidable pair of the earl and the countess.

"Now," Eliza said, "let's have the whole story, Cassandra."

She knew she looked sheepish, because she felt it keenly. "I know we should have told you sooner. It is a bit difficult to explain."

Spencer smiled. "It must have been exciting, this secret investigation. Eliza seems to be forgetting the intrigues we got into before we had to be hosts."

"Oh, no. I have not forgotten." The countess fixed Cassandra with a stern look. "Which is why I know that those two have not been merely investigating."

"It is beside the point now," Spencer said, grinning.

"Moot, in fact," Cassandra said, hearing the sadness in her own voice. "I admit that there was a . . . gratuitous affection—it is over. Now I am concerned for the viscount's welfare. He could be in great danger."

Eliza looked unconvinced.

"Leaving that aside for the moment, exactly what did you find during this little espionage?"

"I inspected Lucy's chambers—and I am sorry, Eliza, I borrowed the master key. But Miss Macallister had leg contraptions of a sort which could be used to make the rapping noises heard at the séance." Cassandra paused. "And a pair of Miles's cuff links."

"The bounder." Spencer shook his head. "I knew it."

"Something must be done there, too," Eliza said.

"The more pressing problem is Lord Thaxton," Cassandra said. "The séance as a hoax is one thing, but the dead bird is quite another."

"It is," Spencer agreed, his hand on the doorknob. "Thank you for your help, Cassandra. I will attend to the viscount's poor humor while you ladies . . . do whatever ladies do when they have to deal with difficult men."

"Tea?" Eliza asked Cassandra, a smile softening her earlier severity. Tea was what ladies did when they had to deal with difficult men.

"Please," Cassandra said.

Once they were safely ensconced in Eliza's sitting room, comfortable and among plates of sweet things and warm tea, the countess dispensed with the formality.

"Did he seduce you?"

"No, no," she said, defensive and altogether suspect, her fingers weak around the teacup. "Not exactly. I cannot say I discouraged it."

"Are you in love?"

"No," she said, an automatic response that felt like a lie. "And neither is he."

A window was open, the breeze tinged with rain. The afternoon had not fulfilled the promise of the morning, which had been a marvel of blue sky.

"Regardless," she added, "I will not marry Miles Markwick."

"Write to your father," Eliza advised. "Perhaps if you tell him that Miles is unfaithful, he will release you from the engagement."

"I considered that, but it will make no difference. Father has been unfaithful for years; he does not think marriage is contingent on fidelity."

"What will you do?"

"I do not know. I certainly cannot go to Lady Dorset and tell her I want out of my engagement. Right now, I intend to find out why Lucy is after Thaxton."

"If she is."

"She is," Cassandra said, a sickening pit blooming in her stomach, "and now I need to know how far she will go."

Chapter Seven

Thaxton paced the library, agitated. He would stay at the house party—but only because Spencer had called in an old debt. When they were nineteen, Thaxton had promised Spencer a forfeit of his choice if he covered for him while he spent the weekend with a special lady (his former governess's sister, in point of fact). Spencer, shrewd devil that he was, had kept that forfeit for ten years and called it in that day.

Miss Seton, Eliza, and Spencer discussed his predicament with little regard to his sulking.

"We cannot assume Miss Macallister did this," Eliza said, her sense of fairness always at the fore. "We certainly cannot outright accuse her."

"She is the prime suspect, then," Cassandra said. "If not her, then who?"

"I do not mean to be indelicate," Eliza said, "but Lord Thaxton is not exactly known for being well liked."

"Thax?" Spencer asked, finally acknowledging his presence. "Can you think of anyone who might have a real vendetta against you?"

He could feel the weight of the letter from his father resting in his jacket pocket. It had arrived in the early afternoon, shortly before this strange meeting of those concerned with his fate.

"You know as well as I do, Spencer, that my reputation is vastly overblown, filled with exaggerations and outright lies. Though I am antisocial, I am not unkind. I can be blunt and no one likes that, but the only person who actively hates me is Markwick. Whoever the culprit is, someone wants to hurt me. I have been thinking of who might have access to my father's notebooks—more to the point, who was in my house after I left for Bath. The wailing woman, the séance, Lucy's arrival . . . it is all working together too perfectly to be a real haunting."

"I am relieved you no longer think a supernatural being is after you," Miss Seton said with a tiny smile.

He ignored her.

"What does the symbol mean?" Eliza asked.

"I know as much as you do on that count—nothing. I do not know its meaning, but I know the Earl Vane is fond of drawing it. It's all over the margins of his notebooks, printed manuscripts, notes to himself. It reoccurs in various forms, some more elaborately decorated, some scrawled. He does a lot of things he does not explain."

"Did you get a letter back from him?" Miss Seton asked, with her wretched knack for asking pertinent questions. He saw Eliza and Spencer look at him—the question also betrayed a certain amount of intimacy. Thaxton crossed his arms and faced a window while Cassandra explained further. "Oh, yes—you do not know about that . . . Thaxton wrote to his father to see if anyone had been to his London estate."

"I did receive a letter," he said, hedging the full truth of the missive, "but the reply was quite morbid and I would rather not share. Suffice it to say, no one has been to see him."

"If we are truly operating in the theory that Miss Macallister did this," Spencer said, sounding as if he was thinking aloud, "then we need to ascertain her motive."

"Tomorrow," Eliza said, sounding a bit more spirited. "We should find some way to interrogate Miles and Lucy separately. They may reveal something to us that they would not to either of you."

"There you are, Eliza." Spencer grinned. "You and Cassandra can spy on the two of them, and Thaxton and I will go over his father's papers."

"We will?" Thaxton asked. "Now we have assignments?"

"Be grateful you are not locked in your room," Spencer said in all seriousness. "Now, I am sure we all have other things to attend to, not the least being dressing for dinner. We can meet tomorrow and regroup."

"You are very handsome when you take charge," Eliza whispered to Spencer as they took their leave.

Thaxton attempted to follow in their footsteps and hide in his room, but a tiny, firm hand stopped him. He turned.

"You are cross because I called off the investigation," Cassandra said.

"Clearly—and you did a horrible job of it. We are very much still investigating, but now you have dragged the Spencers into it."

"You know why I did it." She searched his face, which he kept passive. "Why I called it off. Thaxton, we were mauling each other in a dumbwaiter. We were not investigating Lucy or Miles—we were investigating each other."

"Interesting imagery," he said faintly.

"I thought we should . . . maintain some distance. I have to find a way out of marrying Miles and . . ." She trailed off.

"And?" he prompted.

"And you are not my way out."

"Would that I were, Cassandra, I would be a lucky man."

"You cannot expect to go on as we have been. My reputation would end up dragged through the mud, and you would be saddled with responsibility you do not want."

"I agree that we have been reckless."

"Jonathan, I was so frightened when I thought something had happened to you," she said with feeling. "I was frantic. I felt I had lost my mind."

He fixed her with a look.

"Sorry." She smiled. "Poor phrasing on my part."

The corners of her eyes curved when she smiled. He had to stop noticing things like that. He could not stop the catalog he had of the quirks of her face; he wanted to kiss each of them, and that was no longer an option. Pity he had not done so when he could.

"All things considered," he said, looking away, "I do not think you should be involved any longer."

"It is no longer your choice—the Spencers are a part of it now. It is serious, not some lark of ours. But feel free to ignore me. Or you could cooperate and make it easier on the both of us. Starting with exactly what was in your father's letter—I can tell it distressed you."

"The Earl Vane confirms that no one has been to see him."

"And that is all he said? You called it morbid."

"Miss Seton, you must listen less carefully to what I say and take no stock at all in my words."

"Sound advice. Jonathan—do not reach for that snifter. What else did it say?"

Her words stopped his hand, which he had not realized was drawing near to the library's ever-present brandy.

"If your appetite for misery is that great, then let me hold forth," he said curtly. Thaxton faced her, one hand supporting his weight on the edge of the bar. If she wanted to know how awful his life was, then he would tell her. He felt sure she would look away soon enough. "My father tells me that no one has been to see him, except my mother. Which is impossible, because she is dead."

Cassandra did not move, did not blink.

"I am so sorry, darling," she said.

"It was a long time ago. All the Countess Vanes die young, from what my father says. Another part of my gloomy future." He looked away from her, since she was apparently not going to break his gaze. He spoke toward the window, feigning rampant interest in the rolling hills beyond. "So, you see, Cassandra—I have not snatched you away from Miles, because marriage to me is essentially a pact for an early grave."

A beat passed. He peeked back at her.

"You are serious," she stated with a weird sort of wonder.

"Entirely."

"You cannot marry me because you believe it would kill me."

"Yes. I know how it sounds."

"You . . . believe . . . on top of your own doom, you would doom your future wife? Because of your father's illness, your nebulous family history? Thaxton, you are a smart man. How can you—"

"By all means, reprimand me." He snorted. "That will help."

She stepped forward, altogether too close, close enough that her bodice brushed against his lapels. Her smell made his mind wipe clean—how did it do that? She stood on the tips of her toes and planted a kiss on his cheek, lingering.

"Forgive me," she said into his ear. "You know I do not believe in curses."

He shivered, his hands wanting to pull her into him. But she was already out of his reach, a soft and naughty smile on her face as she exited the room. Thaxton drew in a breath. She, maddening and irresistible, had not shrunk at the idea of marrying him. She had not treated him like he was pitiable. She was not scared, and the knowledge of that left him stunned.

And stirred.

The next afternoon, he stood in that same library, behind a stack of his father's various assorted texts.

"This is all I have," he said to Spencer, patting the top books in the pile with care, lest he topple the whole sheaf. "Mind you, I only thought of a fortnight's stay, not a meaningful study. I have been slowly working my way through this, deciphering, putting accounts to rights. Cannot hire a solicitor to do that, considering everything in his diary. He will note what he had for dinner or who insulted whom at a party in 1866, in the margin of a bill of sale."

Spencer examined the stack.

"Not much to go on," he said. "What are the books at the top?"

"Volumes three and four of the family histories—I have already finished one and two." He opened the leaf of one of the volumes, where the Vane family crest was, including a breakdown of the various parts. He ran a finger over the family motto, *Concussus surgo*. When Struck, I Rise. "The loose papers are unsent correspondence of the Earl Vane. I have to vet it all before it goes to post."

"It would help to know what we are looking for," Spencer said, opening the other volume.

The colors of the mantling—purple and gray—had begun to fade. Thaxton tapped a finger on the coronet above the shield that denoted his earldom.

"I do not know why we are bothering," he said.

"Either way," Spencer said, peering over his shoulder. "There it is."

He drew an invisible circle with his finger, indicating the green knoll at the bottom of the crest. Inside the grass, sure enough, was the symbol repeated in a pattern. It just looked like detail of the grass on first glance, but it was actually the very symbol his father drew, the one that had been rendered on his door gruesomely.

He needed a drink. Instead of having one, he went to lie down.

He sighed, undoing his tie as he returned to his room. Sutton had knotted it far too tightly, and it was beginning to chafe. He would rest and not go to dinner at all, would indulge the luxury of his reputation for being absent.

Miles Markwick ruined his plan, lurking in the foyer of his suite.

"Good evening, Markwick," Thaxton said, tamping down his surprise. "I suggest you say anything you need to say at once, as this will not be happening again."

"Drink, Thaxton?" Miles gestured to the sideboard.

"No, thank you. But do feel free."

"I am glad to see you sobering up," Miles said as Thaxton sat down across from him, their chairs flanking the fireplace. "You were embarrassing yourself."

"I was embarrassing others. Myself, I could not care less. Why are you here, Markwick?"

"To make amends. We will always be at the same parties. It is inescapable."

"Why not go back to Scotland instead? That would fix two of my problems at once."

"It doesn't have to be like this. It seems so senseless for us to be acting like jealous schoolboys—just because your father always liked me better."

Thaxton could not help but laugh.

"Childish nonsense. Are you trying to get a rise out of me? You were eager for any approval at all, and he never liked me much. I doubt the Earl Vane would recognize you at all, dear old cousin Miles. It does not matter any longer."

Miles's smile turned cruel.

"So sour, Thaxton. Look on the bright side—he will forget his wife died bringing forth you, bitter disappointment. You and he can have a new relationship in his senility."

"Get out," Thaxton said, pointing toward the door. "How dare you even approach saying my mother's name. Get out before I remove you myself."

"Ah, not yet. Do you want to introduce the subject of my fiancée, or shall I?"

"A question that is its own answer."

"Have you defiled her?"

Again, the viscount laughed. Miles was easily the most hilarious thing in the entire house party.

"No, indeed. But I wager you have defiled Lucy Macallister. You should have the decency to let Cassandra loose."

"Not a chance," Miles sneered. "I need her dowry, and I can have a mistress. A very fine traditional English marriage. Besides, it serves her right—if my father had known how much those coalfields were worth, I would be wealthy and unsaddled with a wife I do not want."

"You are disgusting. You do not deserve her."

Thaxton hardly knew what he was saying before it had been said, but he did not take it back. He felt the truth of it in his bones.

"Oh, but you do? Deserve her? If that is the case, then let us settle it—pay me twice her dowry and you can have her."

"*Have* her?" Thaxton roared. "I can *have* her? She is not a thing you can sell."

"No deal, then, I suppose. Too bad. It seemed like a very good solution."

Yes, Thaxton thought, it would be a very good solution for him to marry Cassandra. But he would be damned if Markwick benefited from it; he wanted him to suffer as much as possible. Cassandra was not to be bartered—she was a vital, brilliant, beautiful storm of a woman. Her father should not have sold her, and Miles should not have bought her; she should have been able to choose her own fate. Thaxton, feeling the flush rise in his face, came to his senses to find his hands around Miles's throat. He was gurgling.

"Let—go—Thax—"

He tightened his hands instead. It gratified him to see Miles turn red like the devil he was. Thaxton wondered if he squeezed hard enough, would horns sprout?

"You feel powerless, Markwick?" He resisted the urge to slam the worm's head against a wall. "I imagine Miss Seton feels much the same."

He released Miles, or more accurately, he shoved him back into the chair. Thaxton could see the imprints his fingers had made on Miles's neck, and he dearly hoped they turned into bruises. Miles heaved in breaths, the color leaving his face as air came back into his lungs.

"You will not get away with this," he puffed. "I will take it straight to Spencer."

"What will you say to him?" Thaxton asked, folding his hands and feeling a strange peace wash over him. "He knows full well what a vicious prick you are, so tattle away. Now get the hell out of my room."

Miles stood, making a show of dusting himself off.

"We shall see when I tell him you assaulted me. You are an animal, and I no longer feel safe here." He tugged at the bottom of his coat, straightening his back. "If Spencer does not remove you from the premises, I will leave tomorrow. With my bride and her stepmother."

Miles marched out.

Thaxton stood by the fire, and it crackled as he seethed. Sutton appeared with an apology for the imposition, which Thaxton accepted almost as if he had not heard. The anger that thrummed through him was an emotion he had not felt in a long time. It felt righteous.

After the rush of throwing Miles around wore off, the consequences came barreling into his consciousness. Should he tell Cassandra all that had transpired? The odds of her doing something drastic would increase if she knew Miles wanted to whisk her away. Thaxton knew now that he could not take it, could not abide having her wrenched from him. He could not let Lady Dorset pull rank and take her stepdaughter home.

It was time he had a frank talk with Miss Seton.

There was a note on Cassandra's desk:

Labyrinth R, L, R, L. After the meeting. Alone.

Her heart gave a little thrill at the wording, which seemed more intimate, somehow different from the previous notes. She spent extra time on her toilette that night.

Miles had been interminable at dinner; now he was prattling about changes he would make to his father's decrepit estate after they married. It pained Cassandra to see him spending her dowry in his head, fantasizing about a future that revolved around him. Stables, superior breeds of horses, likely to fuel his none-too-secret love of gambling.

Everything had seemed bleak until she saw Thaxton's handwriting. All thoughts of being the dismal Mrs. Markwick, a second fiddle to horses, melted away.

When it came time for the meeting with the Spencers, she and Thaxton arrived first. Much like the night of the séance, they were a little too impatient. Instead of "Good evening" or a nod, he said, "You look lovely."

It took her off guard.

"Thank you," she said belatedly, sitting next to him on the settee. Cassandra felt herself yearning for the days when he was too scruffy, even though it was barely a week ago. Now that he was always all crisp and clean and infuriatingly symmetrical, her hands wanted to touch him. She folded them in her lap. It was either her imagination or his eyes were getting brighter. The blue that had been a colder, grayer hue nowadays seemed lit from behind, softer.

"Miles came to see me," he said with a forced casualness that told her there was far more to the story.

"What did he want?"

"He had a lot to say, but then I choked him."

Spencer and Eliza breezed in with their impeccable timing, both looking the better for having spent the day outside. Eliza had planned a picnic and made sure that there were not any rampant rumors about Thaxton's door.

Cassandra was stuck on Thaxton's last comment—had he been serious? Had he physically choked Miles, or was it a strange metaphorical turn? He noticed her quizzical expression and grinned, which changed his whole face. For a moment, just a moment, she felt dizzy.

"Cassie?" Eliza asked in a tone that indicated it was not the first time she had addressed her friend.

"Sorry—yes?"

"I asked if you felt ill. You look flushed."

"No, no. Thank you. It has been a long day."

She could feel Thaxton's grin stretch.

"As I said," Spencer continued, keeping them on track, "we found the symbol. So that tells us that it is definitely someone who has knowledge of Thaxton's family. We still do not know if anyone has been to Thaxton's home."

"We do," Thaxton said, sliding a letter across the table. When his hand returned to the settee, it curled behind her back. She could feel him stroking, tracing the bottom of her corset, the fabric between the boning, his fingers smoothing it against her skin. "This is a letter I had previously dismissed as my father's ramblings. I had thrown it in the trash. Upon reading it now, I see it is the work of a man entranced—with a blonde woman who had visited him."

"Lucy," Cassandra said, the hitch in her voice twofold—surprise and the effort of speaking while he was touching her. His hand had stilled at her back, present but no longer teasing.

"This proves she had something to do with it, correct?" Eliza asked, taking up the letter.

"Not definitively, but between this and the leg straps we told you about, it seems likely. She will have noticed the straps are missing by now, which explains her increasingly nervous manner."

The countess ruffled the letter open. "My, this is some flowery speech. 'My angel, your perfume lingers.'"

Cassandra could feel Thaxton bristle. "Unkind to use an old man in such a way."

"Do you want her out, Thax?" Spencer turned stony. "Say the word."

"No, I want to know why this is happening. And to do that, we all need to be here."

The surety in Thaxton's voice alarmed Cassandra, because it sounded so new coming from him. He was a man taken to mumbling, moping, and being mostly indecipherable. Yet this sounded like a fresh resolve and made her wonder more about the evening's events. His directions to a spot in the labyrinth were tucked in her shoe. It was as if the air around them glowed iridescent with possibility.

Eliza's eyebrows shot up in tandem, so fast they blurred.

"You two are sitting quite close. Are we no longer polite enough to pretend you are not . . ." She trailed off, searching for an appropriate term. "Carrying on?"

"I like that, Countess," Thaxton said. "It is apt. We are most certainly carrying on."

To her horror, Cassandra's heart did backflips. Hearing him say that, not concerned if Spencer and Eliza knew, started a fluttery feeling in her chest. She had to take a moment before she could speak.

"Well," Eliza said, not willing to go any further down that path, "I am glad you gentlemen had better luck. As for Cassie and I, neither Lucy nor Miles said anything even remotely incriminating."

"Miles was solicitous with me," Cassandra said. "We picnicked. No threats, nothing."

"He saved that for when he showed up in my chambers," the viscount said.

"What?" Eliza said, appalled.

Yes, what? Cassandra's mind demanded.

"After the hunt, Markwick ambushed me in my own room. Said he wanted to make amends, but proceeded to try to sell me Cassandra for the price of her dowry. I also choked him until he could not breathe."

"He tried to *sell* you Cassandra?" Spencer was revolted.

"He did. And gods forgive me, I considered the offer." Thaxton looked over to her, his eyes softening. "If only to be done with it."

"Reprehensible," Eliza spat. "It will not stand."

"I am not surprised by Miles," Thaxton said. "I am, however, impressed that I did not kill him outright."

"Very kind of you." Eliza smiled.

"I will be the one who has to deal with this," Spencer predicted. "Miles will likely ask me to boot you, Thaxton."

"He will, but I would appreciate if you did not." Thaxton glanced over at Cassandra again, troubling her with another of his meaningful glances from heavy-lidded eyes. Eliza was giving her a very different look—the one that translated to "You are playing with fire."

"Good," Spencer said. "I feel the same. And I have an idea. I think we should ask Miss Macallister to hold another séance."

"Brilliant," Cassandra almost gasped. "I wish I had thought of that. It is just the way to see if we can get new information without letting them know we are onto them."

"Also, an effective stalling technique. Miles cannot insist I leave nor can he try to run off with his disobedient bride." Thaxton smiled with satisfaction, and Cassandra could only watch him out of the corner of her eye, for if she met his, she would break into a grin.

"I shall speak with her tomorrow morning," Eliza decided. "She will feel obligated, even if she does not want to do it."

After a few more minutes of planning, they retired. When Thaxton kissed her hand to make a show of saying good night, secret promise lurked in his gaze.

"See you soon," he murmured.

Goose bumps rose on her arms.

Thaxton waited around the final turn of the directions he had given Cassandra. When she rounded the corner, he pulled her into his arms before she could protest. He caught her little yelp with his mouth, swallowed it with a kiss.

"Thaxton," she said on a breath, "you scared me."

He nipped her bottom lip; he could not resist. If she insisted on talking, they could damn well talk and kiss at the same time.

"They do call me the Ghost, dear. Boo."

He bent to take her again. Meeting in the labyrinth had seemed mysterious and dreamy, but now he felt he should have chosen a place where there was somewhere to lie down. The longer the embrace went on, the more his hands roved, the more hers did, he coveted a bed or a settee or any surface that was not the damp ground of the hedge maze. Yet if they had a soft place to land, the situation would get entirely out of hand.

Cassandra pulled her head back. Her face was flushed, and her eyes had the too-bright glow of lust. Thaxton kept his arms around her, encircling. There was no reason for him to hold himself back anymore, or pretend he did not want her. Miles had pushed him to the very point of his patience, and now Thaxton had no guilt at all about. If Miles already thought he was trying to steal his fiancée, then he was damn well going to do it.

"I know you did not call me here just to kiss," she said.

"Mostly to kiss. Some talking." He nuzzled her cheek, leaving a small peck in his wake.

"Did you really choke Miles?"

"Indeed, I did," he said slowly, seeing that the idea pleased her, though she was fighting the feeling. He pulled her closer, tightening his arms around her waist so that they were closer than they had ever been, coiled. "I throttled him. I am not sorry."

"Still," she hedged as he traced his lips along her jawline, "you should not have done that."

"I know," he rumbled against her neck, feeling her shiver, "but it felt so good."

"Jonathan," she sighed.

That husky release of his name was enough to drown any other words; he could not hear anything above the roar in his ears created by her embrace. He knew in a swoop of a feeling like blue light that he loved her. Knew that what he was about to do was what needed to be done. He could start to change things. Cassandra forced him to imagine a future, because he could not conceive of her existing and not being his.

Reluctantly, he pulled back.

"Pardon me for a moment," he said in a low voice crafted not to intrude on the moment, on the sacred silence of the night and the wind in the trees. He turned, going toward the corner of one of the hedge walls.

Thaxton was sure the box would be where he had buried it. Why would anyone ever check between the hedges in the maze after a right, then left, another right, and a left? The physical location held a specific spot in the labyrinth of his mind as well, the place where he left his soul locked. He parted the hedge with some effort and knelt, examining the small space coiled with foliage. A tiny bit of light shone in, but he could not see very well. He did not need to. He ran his hands over the ground, finding the mound without any trouble. It took him a few moments before he could have a visible effect on the dirt—something that he should have thought through. Why had he not brought a gardening shovel? His hands were filthy by the time his fingers hit the cedar box.

"Jonathan?" Cassandra's voice asked, perplexed.

"Sorry," he said, emerging with the tiny relic in his hand. Leaves and twigs clung to him, pieces of the hedge. When he tried to brush them off, he got dirt everywhere—on his jacket, in his hair. Fantastic. He was going to propose to Cassandra covered in dirt and greenery. She was staring at him.

He took a breath.

"I suppose that I am about to tell you something very personal," he said, in a sort of awe that he *wanted* to tell her. "But you already know a lot of things that should have made you run the other way, yet you did not."

She smiled in a tentative way, like he was an animal she did not want to scare.

"Are you saying you trust me?"

"Inasmuch as I trust anyone."

"What is that?" she said, looking suspiciously at his hand. "You are covered in mud."

"It requires some explanation. Two years ago, my father began deteriorating in earnest. It took a while until he was incapable of being in public, but before that he was acting very strangely at home. Sometimes to me, sometimes to the servants. It was as if he was fading in and out. He had outbursts."

She was listening, not trying to interject, not even nodding. He was not sure that anyone had ever done that for him, listened without trying to sympathize or patronize him.

"You know my mother is dead, but I do not think I told you that she died birthing me. I never knew her, but people say she and my father were very much in love. In a lot of ways, he never got over losing her, so I lost him as well."

She did not interrupt.

"I digress. As I said, two years ago the Earl Vane was increasingly taking leave of his senses. One evening, he decided that he wanted none of my mother's possessions in the house. He insisted that I get rid of her wedding ring. He wanted me to throw it into the Thames."

"No," she breathed.

"That had better not be pity on your brow, Cassandra."

"Never," she said. "I am dismayed."

He struggled with the latch on the box.

"I could not do it." The rust on the latch held it closed and he had to force it, another inelegant movement. He had imagined the scene much less awkward, himself much more gallant. "I buried it here, I cannot tell you why, I do not know. I could have placed it in safekeeping, but I was convinced my father would find out that I had kept it. Mind you, Cassandra, I did not put it here because I thought *I would* ever need it."

He flipped open the lid. His mother's ring gleamed—his father had polished it lovingly before he abandoned it. It glowed the same way it had the night Thaxton had put it in the ground. The sapphire caught the moon and smashed it to pieces, throwing shards of light in a starburst around it. Cassandra had stilled even more.

He took her hand, not dropping to one knee because he felt he needed to look her in the eye. Too late, he remembered he was covered in soil, but there was no choice but to push through.

"Cassandra, we are out of time," he said. "Miles will speak with your mother, and then you will be gone."

"I have to run away," she said, jerking her hand.

He held it tighter, the ring clutched in his other hand.

"I have an idea, hence the long story and the ring." Thaxton took a deep breath. "Will you let me ruin you, Cassandra Seton, and therefore marry me?"

"What?"

Oh, he had definitely phrased that wrong. His automatic reaction, again, the wrong one, was to push the ring at her in a frantic manner.

"You cannot get out of your engagement but for one circumstance—your reputation compromised. Being that my own reputation is sullied, I can assure you that it is nowhere as bad as it seems. It is freeing." Cassandra gaped at him, the ring box wedged between their bodies. "Spend the night with me. I will make sure we are discovered in the morning, and we can marry in a blaze of scandal."

"That is—"

"Mad?" he finished for her.

"We will be pariahs," she said.

"Nonsense. We will be invited everywhere. We will be a spectacle. I can handle it. Can you? Cassie, please, will you?"

She looked at him, somewhere between puzzled and shocked. He did not break her gaze, though he wanted to. It was too piercing, like her thoughts were manifesting as fog, weighing on him.

"No," she said.

In Cassandra's experience, men never decided they loved you in a swooping fashion while also worshipping your power and grace. They wanted you for practical purposes, such as your money or their honor. Cassandra Seton was growing mightily tired of proposals that did not include the word "love." She had been the recipient of two such proposals thus far, and neither of them satisfied her.

In Thaxton's case, she assumed it was honor.

"Did you say no?" the viscount sputtered, as if it were inconceivable.

"Yes, Jonathan. No."

He stepped back, taking the ring away with his hands.

"I am offering you a way out," he said, his voice too even. "I know that ruination will be an unsavory way to do so—"

"Stop," she said.

He was offering her a way out, he said. Not happiness, mutual affection, or a family. A way out.

"You feel obligated," she said. "And I think a little sorry for me."

He had a pained look on his face, his features drawn taut.

"I feel—strongly, Cassandra."

"I see that," she said, and she truly did. She could tell he was sincere in his desire to help her, which hurt more. She did not want his help; she wanted his love. She tried to keep her voice formal. "It is noble of you, but no thank you."

"Mucked it up, did I not?" he said.

Yes, she thought but did not say.

"Darling," he said, clutching her hand again, pulling her in, "I know I made a muddle of that, but I am sincere. Please—marry me."

"You said yourself that you are unsuitable."

She shifted in his arms.

"I have changed my mind. Thoroughly." He pressed the ring into her palm and closed her fingers around it. "Think about it. We work well together, do we not?"

Another turn of phrase that seemed too realistic. They worked well together; they did not burn with a passion that must be answered. Cassandra pressed her lips together, fighting the urge to tell him what she was thinking. The blue light of the labyrinth made him every inch the dark hero as he held her, all shadowed cheekbones, and damn him, it should have been romantic.

She drew in a breath for strength.

"I think you will look back on this and regret it. We have not even known each other a month."

"You met Miles twice before this trip. You and I have had more conversation; I am certain of it. Besides, it had not occurred to me how long we have been acquainted." He paused, searching her eyes. "Do you not feel . . . ?"

He did not finish the sentence, the remnants of his last word searching fruitlessly for the next. She thought for a moment that he was going to say it; it being, *I love you and I must have you.*

"Cassandra," he said, his jaw tight, "I dug my mother's ring out of the ground for you. What more do you want to prove my earnestness?"

What an idiot she was for wanting three silly words. He was right that his actions spoke far louder, but there was a roar in her for verbal clarity. She felt stupid and childish, but she could not shake it. She wanted to hear it, wanted to hear him say he wanted her, outside of his wish to save her from Miles.

"Thaxton, you have spent most of our acquaintance trying to impress upon me how you can never marry."

Cassandra hated the way she sounded. She wanted to go back, start over. Even if he never loved her, it was a better fate than being Mrs. Markwick. It was probably a better fate than trying to make her way alone, penniless and outcast. Thaxton would never mistreat her, and the bedroom would be exhilarating. He might grow to love her. But would he want her to have babies? She was not sure she wanted to be in the heir-making business, considering the trouble that being a Vane heir entailed.

"If it helps, I was reading my family histories, and my father was mistaken about the Countesses Vane. Not all of them die young. I think that may be something he twisted to suit his inner world after losing my mother."

"I had not even pondered the curse," she said, not altogether truthfully. It would not do to have him think she was buying into it, even thinking of it.

"Rest assured that it would not kill you to marry me. But, according to the rest of the history, a case could be made for the majority of what my father calls the curse. Add that to your catalog of reasons we should not wed; then decide in favor of marriage anyway."

"I will take it into consideration," she said, somewhat wryly.

"Please do." He picked up her hand again, tracing his finger around her palm as he had at the séance table. It set her every nerve on end, but then he raised his eyes to her, and she discovered nerves that had no scientific name. "And then if it is ruin that you choose, madam, I will bring cities down at your feet."

She amended what she thought earlier about his proposal. Maybe it was a bit romantic. Cassandra hoped she was not gaping at him, but he had honestly robbed her of words. It was disconcerting as she was never at a lack of them.

"I do not think I should debase myself by asking you again," he said, taking her silence as a firm no. His posture slumped.

A contrary panic seized her—was she losing her chance with him? The thought terrified her far more than she would have liked.

"Give me a day," she blurted. "One day to think about it."

"Take as long as you need," he said, tilting his head to kiss her again.

It seemed much easier than talking; their kisses could not be misinterpreted. His hands on her cheeks brought back the sense memory of their first kiss in the dim blue parlor, when she had been so bold.

The more she kissed him, the more she thought she would endure anything as long as it quenched what he awakened in her every time they came together.

Even now, when he only touched her with one hand, he was too creative. The empty ring box stayed clutched in one hand while the other had traveled to her bottom, crushing her against him. Cassandra tightened her fist on the ring, her other arm at his neck, fingers snaking into his hair. She felt him growing harder against her, and desire hit her so strong it frightened her. She let out a little moan, barely recognizing her own voice. Thaxton actually growled.

"We must stop," he said with very little breath. "I would like nothing more than to ruin you, but I must insist on a bed."

For a moment she considered suggesting ruination take place that very night, and damn the consequences.

So Cassandra led with that when she got to Eliza's door.

"He wants to ruin me," she said, "and I want to let him."

The countess was already in her nightclothes, but she did not look too shocked to see her friend. She ushered her in and handed her a glass of brandy without asking. Cassandra took it, and followed Eliza's lead in sitting by the low fire. The countess treated her gingerly, and she appreciated it.

She took a drink, then opened her palm, the sapphire glinting in the light.

"He also asked me to marry him."

"I fail to see an issue. Besides the scandal, do you not love him?"

"I do," she said, closing her hand around the ring again. "But he does not love me."

Eliza let a beat pass before answering.

"Of course he does," she said with a short laugh. "He just neglected to say."

She made it sound so logical. Cassandra took another drink, quaffing the brandy, with a thought in the back of her mind that she had been drinking more than Thaxton lately. "I need to hear it," she said, setting the now-empty glass down. "I know it does not make sense."

"It makes perfect sense," Eliza replied. "You did not get that with Miles; he did not even get you a ring. You want to make sure this is different. That it is for the right reasons."

"Exactly." Eliza put it into words better than she had mustered. Cassandra stood, holding her arms out to her friend. "I am sorry to barge in on you."

She smiled and hugged her. "Anytime. But get some sleep now."

"You, too."

Before closing the door, Eliza patted her arm.

"He will pull up to scratch. I feel it."

Chapter Eight

"Honestly, Lord Spencer," Miles said the next morning. His spinelessness surrounded him like a gas as he paced forward in the study. "You cannot allow his disgraceful actions to go unpunished."

Spencer, looking official behind his desk, glanced at Thaxton with obvious annoyance. "I am sorry, Mr. Markwick. But sending Thaxton home is quite out of the question."

Thaxton, he of the disgraceful actions, lounged on the side sofa. He was rather pleased with those disgraceful actions, so he could endure Miles's bloviating. Miss Seton had nearly accepted his unorthodox proposal, and if that happened, none of this rot mattered.

"I do hate pulling rank," he said in a bored, aristocratic tone he knew would annoy Miles, "but Markwick leaves me no choice. If anyone should be punted, it is he."

"Hardly," Miles scoffed. "You are a danger to Spencer's entire house party—violent and unpredictable. There is also the matter of the rumored dead raven with a slit throat on your balcony."

"Hmm. And how do you know that?" Thaxton gave him a slow smile. "Because you did it or because of a little bird called Lucy?"

Miles stepped toward him. "Are you accusing me?"

"And Lucy, yes."

"Gentlemen," Spencer said, hiding his amusement behind a grimly set face, though he could not keep it out of his voice, "now is not the time for quibbling. As Markwick pointed out, this household is in danger. But it seems to me that our good Lord Thaxton is the victim here, do you not think? The events surrounding him as of late have been detrimental to his temper. Certainly we can forgive him a momentary lapse in judgment."

Thaxton knew he indeed had made a lapse in judgment, but it had not been choking Miles. That was justified and he would not regret it. He did, however, regret the way the night before had transpired. He did not know why he had frozen when he tried to tell Miss Seton he loved her. He suspected it had to do with the fact that he had little to no experience in loving anyone, much less verbalizing it. He loved Spencer and his father, but there was no need to go about announcing it. But Cassandra had been waiting for him to say it, and he could not.

He should have just seduced her.

"I am disappointed, Lord Spencer," Miles pronounced. "I thought you would see my point. There is little other solution but for me to repair to the Marquess of Dorset's estate with Miss Seton in tow. I am sure Lady Dorset will agree."

"I doubt Cassie would like that," Thaxton said, savoring Miles's simmering rage. "In fact, I know she would not."

"Allow me to steer us back to shore," Spencer said, crossing to the front of his desk so that his presence was the largest in the room. He put himself conveniently between the other two men. "Miles, you know about the symbol on Thaxton's door, so you must realize we have a larger issue than one altercation."

"Yes, the issue that my deranged cousin painted a door with animal's blood? I agree, my lord, that is a bigger problem."

Thaxton did not bother to defend his own honor.

"Not but a week ago, you believed in otherworldly events," Spencer said. "Can you not conceive that Thaxton may be the one in peril here?"

Miles's face scrunched, searching for a way out of the question, a hole in it to squish through.

"Of course, I would never deny Spiritualism," was all he could come up with.

"Lucy Macallister seems to agree." Spencer could not resist a little smile, the same that he always wore when he had the advantage in a fencing match. Thaxton had seen it many a time from behind a sword. "She will be doing another séance this evening. We were hoping, Miles, that you and Cassandra would stay for continuity. We were all at the first sitting; it should be the same with the second."

"One more night cannot possibly hurt," Thaxton said with forced innocence. "You can leave with your blushing bride on the morrow."

Or, he added inwardly, *she will wake up in my bed, and then I will abscond with her.* That hinged on her answer. He had not been able to use the correct words, but he thought he had made his desire rather apparent. In more ways than one. Yet still she could refuse.

"One more night," Miles grumbled. "I am through with parlor games and do not intend to stay in a place where I have been both assaulted and accused." He glared at Thaxton again. "But you stay away from me, Viscount. More importantly, you stay away from Cassandra."

"Understood," Thaxton said. It was not a lie—he understood, he was just not willing to comply.

"The blue room at midnight," Spencer said. "Now both of you get out of my study, I have work to do."

Thaxton did not know what work Spencer could possibly have to do at the moment, but he was glad to divest himself of Miles's presence.

He discovered Eliza lurking outside the door to Spencer's study. She could have been listening. Miles passed her without a glance, not seeing the countess for as fast as he skittered out of the room.

"Lord Thaxton," she greeted him, sounding more amenable than ever before. It dawned on Thaxton that he and the countess had never before spoken one-on-one. "I was hoping you might take a turn in the garden."

"Would you call me Jonathan?" He gave her his most nonthreatening smile and offered his arm. "I assume Cassandra has spoken to you. That would be why you seek an audience with me."

The countess nodded, putting her hand in the crook of his arm. They reached the verdant area at the front of the larger garden, equipped with a path for casual wanderers. They strolled at a leisurely pace, the sun bright and high.

"Are you sincere?" she said after a long time. "In your affections for her?"

"Utterly. Though I am never sure of anything," he admitted, "Cassandra is the exception. I have no doubt that we could make each other happy."

"Then consider this a courtesy. My Cassie is an incurable romantic, Jonathan, though she does not want the world to know it. I should not be telling you this, you must appreciate, but it was a real mistake to not declare your devotion. She believes you want to bed her and also play the hero, but not that you love her."

"Clearly I love her," he said, finding it much easier to say when Cassandra was not in the room. "I nearly told her so."

"But you did not."

"Neither did she!"

She had not, though it felt puerile for him to perceive a sting in that. He had spent a moment with his breath held during the proposal, thinking she was going to say it. Thinking, *Surely she will say it now*. It would have been easier for him to parrot it back, knowing that she had already revealed her hand. She had not.

"Percival botched his proposal, too," Eliza said, fondness in her expression. "He asked me directly after an indiscretion. I thought it impulsive."

"He told me," Thaxton said, happy to have the other side of that story available to her. "He came to my house after you said you needed time. He was very scared, but do not tell him I told you that. We fenced for over an hour, but his panic would not abate."

"Silly man," she said, shaking her head. "He knew I wanted to accept."

"Does Cassandra? Because I will not impose it on her again if you do not think she is agreeable."

Eliza pressed her lips together. "She is. But I did not tell you that."

"Thank you," he said, meaning it deeply.

"You and I barely know each other, my lord, but I have never seen my friend so . . . agitated. It will be very easy to make this right."

He nodded, noticing that they had returned to the garden entrance. The countess must have had hundreds of garden talks to hone her timing to such precision.

She bowed her head. "Until this evening, Lord Thaxton. And if it turns out you need someone to discover you *in flagrante delicto*, do send me a note."

Thaxton watched her walk back inside, not believing his ears. Somehow, he had gotten the go-ahead from both of the Spencers. It had to be a miracle.

Even if there were no spirits in Spencer House, something supernatural was afoot.

❧☙

Cassandra stayed in her room until three minutes before midnight. She had no wish to arrive early this time, to be faced with Thaxton alone. During dinner, he shamelessly smoldered in her direction, his gaze saying things that had no place at a meal. The only option had been to keep her head down and attempt to be demure, which was something she struggled with on a good day. Miles spent dinner a single word away from an outburst as it was.

When she reached the blue parlor, everyone was already seated, waiting for her. Thaxton, who somehow managed to appear both stately and infuriatingly dissolute, gave a half smile.

"You are late," Miles reprimanded. "I hope it is because you were packing your trunks."

She had been nearly packed for days, though not as he'd desired. One traveling bag whittled down to essentials. A bag that she could carry alone, the essentials of her existence. A plan for an emergency.

"I apologize," Cassandra said compactly. "Let us get this over with, shall we?"

Eliza bristled visibly. Cassandra knew the lack of emotional discretion being displayed would make her friend uneasy, but she could no longer pretend she felt anything toward Miles but scorn. She sat down next to the countess, flanked on the other side by Lucy. They had discussed the seating in depth, in order to best detect any suspicious activity from the medium or Miles. Thaxton sat on the other side of Lucy, next to Spencer. The seating, practical as it was, also assured Cassandra that she would not have to be next to Thaxton. She was not ready to be that near to him.

The note she had received an hour before in his decisive hand read, *Eschew the labyrinth tonight. Come to my room.* She had not been able to think since.

Thaxton smiled across the table from her. It looked as if he could read her thoughts, and he did not dislike playing the reprobate.

"Thank you for attending us again, Lucy," he said with uncharacteristic graciousness. Apparently Thaxton was in a generous mood. "I, especially, appreciate the use of your talents again, given my unique position."

"I am happy to help where I can," she said, looking down. She seemed much more anxious in comparison to the first séance, when she had been so self-assured. Cassandra almost felt sorry for her, but then she remembered that no matter what, the target of this ruse had been Thaxton. That was an unforgivable offense.

"If you will all join hands again," Lucy said with an air of resignation. "And do close your eyes."

The bell was under the jar in the middle of the table, but all the rest of the accoutrements had been abandoned. No more stones or rose petals; the room more brightly lit on Eliza's insistence. It served to take away all the atmosphere. Only one of them joined Lucy in shutting her eyes: Miles. The rest of the party looked at each other in expectation.

"Honored spirit," Lucy continued in hollow tones, "we have come together tonight to ask humbly that you make your presence known again. Please ring the bell if you wish to communicate."

She did not go through the bit about rapping; of course she did not. She no longer had her contraptions. Cassandra looked over at Thaxton, who raised his tediously perfect eyebrow. It had been easier to evade him when they first met, with his confidence shaken and mind scrambled. The unpleasant side effect of helping him, she now knew, was that Thaxton at his full strength was too much for her to bear. No longer drifting along, his new certainty brought back his charm. There would be no denying him anything, no matter how foolhardy.

And by god, he looked gorgeous in candlelight.

"If you are here, please ring the bell once," Lucy said, her breathing uneven and her eyes shut too tight. The bell rang, not a strong ring, but one tiny flicker.

"She moved," Thaxton mouthed to Cassandra, inclining his head at the medium. He turned and repeated it to Spencer, who nodded.

She had indeed moved—Cassandra could not tell if it had been her left or right foot. It was definitely her foot, since her hands had remained still. Amazingly, her legs had not moved either. Whatever she was doing required a fair amount of skill and practice. Spencer's gaze traveled around the table, trying to detect anything amiss, and Eliza watched Miles so intently that it was a wonder he did not feel her scrutiny.

"Spirit," Lucy said, her voice faltering, "we seek information regarding the entity attached to Lord Thaxton. Can you help?"

There was no movement, no sound, nothing but their four pairs of eyes, watching and waiting. Miles let out a breath, and the candles wavered.

"Should I go into another trance?" Lucy asked with uncertainty. Cassandra did not like her posture at all. She had shrunk into herself, making it evident that she was no longer enjoying the role.

"I have a question," Thaxton said, "if I might."

"Of course," Lucy said, though it sounded more like *Please don't*.

Cassandra prayed that Thaxton would ask a question that could be answered with a no. If Lucy had to ring the bell twice more, Cassandra thought she would be able to detect the deception. She caught his gaze, and the table between them might have caught on fire with the heat of it. He slanted his mouth down—an absolutely delicious mouth, she noted.

"Honored spirit," he said with all seriousness, "is Miles Markwick in love with Cassandra Seton?"

Jonathan Vane, king of the loaded question.

Lucy's hand tightened on Cassandra's, likely the viscount's as well. Her whole body went rigid, but not as it had in the trance. The question did not sit well with anyone at the table, least of all the medium. She started trembling a bit, her eyes shut even tighter as if she could block out the whole room. Eliza showed the first sign of worry, and Miles's eyes had opened a crack.

Below them, a bell sounded, but there was no ring. It sounded as if it had hit the ground and rolled. It was not an answer from a spirit; it was a mistake. Cassandra felt the floor around her with her foot, and the bell tinkled.

"Aha!" she exclaimed, unable to mask her triumph. She darted below the table, seized the bell and Lucy's boot—of course, she had taken it off so that she could ring the bell with her toes, how clever—and plunked them both on top of the table. They all dropped hands.

And stared at her.

Cassandra did not feel like a hero in the moment. She stood over the dainty boot and bell, and no one applauded. No one even spoke.

Lucy looked mortified, not like a villain being revealed. She had gone sheet white. An angry flush crept down Miles's neck. Eliza and Spencer had both folded their hands, waiting to see what would happen. When Cassandra's eyes finally found Thaxton's again, she saw gentle reproach. *Badly done, and you know it.*

"Good lord," Miles said, stuffing his tone full of appalled shock. "Miss Macallister, how could you deceive us this way?"

"Pah," Thaxton said, frowning. "You have no shame."

"Miles?" Lucy's voice was small, a plea, filled with disappointment that she could not keep inside any longer. It hung in the air until Thaxton put a hand on her arm.

"It is over, Miss Macallister. If you do not want to protect him anymore, don't." He spoke as an aside to Lucy, not for the whole group. "You can tell us if he made you do this."

She did not answer him. She did not even make any indication she had heard him.

Spencer rose, the scrape of his chair followed closely by his wife's. They both stood, lending finality to the situation.

"I am afraid," Spencer said in a voice closer to his late father's than his, "that we will have to make some painful decisions tomorrow morning."

Lucy's eyes brimmed with tears. She looked once more toward Miles, who refused to meet her gaze. She picked up her boot and stomped from the room, one foot bare. Cassandra felt another twinge of sympathy. Something was very wrong here.

"Of course, Lord Spencer," Miles said, his gaze following the medium's retreat, "and we would all understand if you wanted to send for Lucy's carriage immediately."

"You are odious," Thaxton said, deadpan. "We shall see if you wish to revise that statement when your Lucy tells us the whole story tomorrow."

"Lucy is not mine," Miles spat. He pointed a finger at Cassandra, stabbing it in her direction. "*She* is mine."

Thaxton was on his feet in a moment, putting his body between Miles's finger and Cassandra. "She is not property, and I suggest you step back."

"Gentlemen," Eliza said, knowing when a female voice was needed to inject sense, "that will be all. It is late, and we can hardly resolve this in so high a temper."

"I will expect everyone in my study at 10:00 a.m.," Spencer said, fixing them all with a stern look. "Do not make me come looking for you."

The earl and countess left in their regal cloud, and Miles seized Cassandra's arm.

"I will see you to your room," he snarled. Cassandra saw Thaxton's hands curl, but he did not move.

"Good night, Lord Thaxton," she said, trying to shove as much meaning as she could into the words, to convey that she would come to him.

"Do not speak to him," Miles snapped, yanking her out of the room and fairly dragging her up the stairs. He kept ranting as they walked. "We will be leaving as soon as possible. As soon as you are in your room, I will go to Lady Dorset and tell her that I caught you with Thaxton. I know it is a lie; I do not care. I have positively had enough of your disrespect."

"I had enough of yours eight years ago." She could no longer even feign politeness to him, nor did he merit it.

"A wicked tongue will not help," he said, his face twisted with ugly anger. "Protest all you want, but you belong to me. I can keep you locked in your room for the rest of your godforsaken life."

"You underestimate my capacity to make you equally unhappy," she retorted, halting outside her door. "Good night, Mr. Markwick. We are not yet wed, so I must ask that you return to your room."

He pointed a finger in his face; evidently he pointed a lot when he was furious.

"I will retrieve you at eight in the morning. There will be hell to pay if you are not here."

Cassandra might have argued longer, but she was smiling to herself, since she knew something that Miles did not. She watched him trounce off; then she spoke into the silence, unable to hide the amusement she felt.

"Thax? You may come out now."

⚜

Thaxton rounded the corner, his mouth slanted.

"You knew I was here?"

"I heard you lean against the wall. Must you lean on everything? It is like you cannot bear to hold yourself upright." He could hear the repressed laughter in her whisper. "I was going to meet you in your room, you know. You did not have to follow us."

"I could not very well leave you alone with that scoundrel."

She opened the door and gestured inside. "Quick."

She did not need to repeat herself; he was in her room in two steps. She closed and locked the door. Thaxton spun around, taking in the room, his eyes settling on the bed. He felt a little drunk, though he had not had a drop.

"How scandalous," he said.

"This is not an invitation," she said, sitting in a chair beside the fire, the dim room and soft light making her glow like an unearthly creature. "We could not keep talking in the hallway."

He found himself unsure where to begin.

"What do you think will happen?" she said, in a very general way. "Tomorrow."

"Spencer will decide it is best to keep this within estate walls, and he will send Lucy Macallister away. I dare not speculate on anything else." He looked down at her hands, empty of adornment. "Where is my mother's ring?"

She clutched the chain on her neck and pulled it out of her bodice. The ring hung there from a delicate silver loop. Thaxton did not want to ask directly if she had made a decision, since he was afraid of the answer.

"It was safer . . ." She smiled at him, a bit saucily, considering where it had been nestled. He would like to be that safe, he thought.

"Keep it, no matter your answer," he said. "It is better than it being in the ground, and it belongs with you."

Same as my heart.

"Whatever my answer, it must be tonight. Miles will find a way to persuade Lady Dorset to leave on the morrow, I am sure." She folded her hands, a worrisome gesture. "And it might be best if I capitulate."

"Not amusing, Cassandra."

"I do not jest. We know that Miles was plotting against you, so it would make sense that I should get him as far away from you as possible. That means my parents' estate, under the watchful eye of my father. It should have occurred to me earlier, but I selfishly wanted . . ."

"What, darling?"

"To stay with you."

"Then stay with me." He leaned forward, clasping his hands solemnly around hers. "I can no longer conceive of a day without you."

When she did not speak, he decided he would have to make her decision clear. He sank to his knees at the foot of the chair and began to untie the ribbons on her absurdly elaborate shoes.

"What exactly are you doing?" she asked in a rush of words as his fingers explored her ankle, delightfully pointy and sheathed in a stocking.

"It is late," he purred. "The ladies' maids are all asleep. There is no one to help you undress."

"I . . ." she started while he divested her of her left shoe.

He held up a hand. "No, you must not protest. I am more than happy to oblige. You simply cannot sleep in that gown. For one, it is too expensive. But moreover, I want you to be comfortable."

Thaxton's hand traveled up Cassandra's left leg. He found the top of the stocking and peeled it off.

"Comfortable?" she said, her voice hoarse. "I have never been so tense in my life."

"Momentarily. Give me time." He moved to the other leg, plunking her shoe on the ground. He repeated the roll of the stocking, taking far too long. "But I promise by the end of the night, you will have never been so relaxed."

He scaled up the chair, seeing how nervous she was and wanting to reassure her before he got too worked up to do so. The slow undressing was proving to be just as difficult for him; his senses were rapidly fleeing from any kind of logic.

"I am waiting on an answer," he said, trailing his fingers up her arm to pull off the long glove. "I will take my time helping you undress. While you think."

She did not speak, but looked at him with impossibly wide eyes. He smiled and kissed her, trying to put every ounce of feeling into it, to convey the feeling he was failing to put into words. The séance had not been a vision of the future, but she was. When he paused to gaze at her, he thought she had never looked more beautiful.

"Your back, please," he whispered, smiling against her cheek.

"Jonathan," she said wispily, turning her back to him even as she protested, "this is not helping me think."

"It will. Allow me to undo these laces very, very slowly, respecting every inch of the fine fabric, and enumerate the reasons you should marry me."

Cassandra shivered when the tips of his fingers touched the sensitive skin at her neck. He twirled a curl around his finger and released it, watching it spring back.

"I do think you are being unfair," she said, strained. It sounded like she was suppressing a moan, and it instantly made him hard.

"Fair?" he asked, twining one single finger at the top of the bodice, working the knot loose. "I know of no rules for this. This is an illustration of the first reason you should marry me." The intricate knot fell open, two ends of the ribbon dangling. He trailed one end along her neck.

"Which is?"

"I want you desperately."

She made a little noise of pleased surprise when he put his lips where the ribbon had been, dawdling. He tilted his head so that he could reach her collarbone, and his tongue traced the side of it. He felt her sharp intake of breath, felt it from the very bottom of her back. He pulled the ribbons through the first few loops, exposing a mere inch of skin, and then her thin chemise traitorously interrupted his full view. Thaxton closed his eyes for a moment—he was losing track of himself already. He inhaled deeply. He had bungled the proposal. He would not repeat the performance now.

"The second reason," he said, releasing a few more loops. "The second reason is a bundle of many. You are composed when needed, impulsive when necessary, thoughtful, gorgeous, and perhaps smarter than I."

"Perhaps?" She smiled over her shoulder.

"Perhaps. Reason the third. You challenge me." Thaxton found that the bodice was loose enough to pull down and felt there was no time like the present. He cupped her breasts from behind, pressing himself into her back. "And I like challenging you."

Finally, the smallest and sweetest moan escaped her.

"You will notice none of these reasons include saving you." He turned her around, cradling her. "I am not in the business of that, madam. Let it be known that I want to steal you, not save you."

"Oh," she said, not an assent, but a reaction to what his thumb was doing to her nipple through the chemise. He kissed her again, introducing his tongue into it as he busied himself with the buttons on the hip of her skirt.

She was holding back, he could tell. He pulled back but kept her tightly in his arms, her body aroused and edgy in equal parts. It made him love her more, but if she did not unwind, it would spoil the experience, and he needed it to be flawless.

Thaxton took off his jacket and laid it on the back of the very crowded chaise longue. He pulled his flask out of an inside pocket. He had not used it lately, but it felt like a small comfort to have it there, a last vestige of all his fears.

He handed it to Cassandra.

"You need to stop thinking," he said.

"You want me to drink?" She gaped at him. "I could not."

"You could. It will help."

Cassandra stared at him for another moment before taking the flask. As she unscrewed the cap, the metal scraping seemed to fill the whole room. She smelled it and wrinkled her nose. "What is this? Whisky?"

"The very finest."

She did not take her eyes off him as she took a sip. He immediately knew it was too dainty and slow. Her eyes watered and she coughed.

"Good lord," she wheezed.

"Take a bigger swig. And more quickly. You should not sip . . . it makes it worse. After a few, it will not seem as horrible."

"Are you still drinking?"

"No, I am not. You are."

⌘

Cassandra figured if she was going to be dissolute and debauched, she ought to go all the way. She took a quick and deep pull from the flask and winced. Horrible. She put back another swig quickly, before her burning mouth could recover. No better. How did people do this all the time? Why would have Thaxton done this to himself, ever?

"One more," Thaxton said. He was watching her with a serene smile, which seemed odd. She felt warm, even though she was half-undressed.

"I feel like I could breathe fire."

"Good, good. Exactly as you should."

She braved one more, because she did like the warm feeling. It did not matter that she was down to her chemise, the top half of her gown dropped almost to her knees. She smiled, absently taking another drink. She tilted her head, watching Thaxton. He really was a beautiful man. If one wanted to be swept off one's feet, he was a fine candidate.

"I fancy you," she said. This time the whisky did not burn so much as slide down her throat. "Jonathan. Jonathan. Your name is lovely, you know."

"That is enough, dear," he said, taking back the flask.

The man had exquisite hands. Giant hands. Hands that were scooping her up and actually, in reality, sweeping her off her feet. Her gown barely stayed on as he lifted her, depositing her gently against the pillows on the bed. She watched as he pulled the garment the rest of the way off and laid it gently over a chair. The air hit her chemise and she shivered. The whole situation had taken on a dreamlike quality.

"I know what happens," she said, her voice wavering. "I am not an idiot."

He quirked an eyebrow. "Pardon?"

"I know what happens in bed, I mean. I have been told."

"Ah," he said, lying down next to her. "Wonderful."

Though he spoke with no particular inflection, his smile turned wolfish. His talented fingers had found their way under the chemise, dancing at the sensitive skin of her inner thighs. The look in his eyes had changed—it had a new glaze, a directionless yearning.

Directionless yearning? She *was* drunk.

"You are far too clothed," she said. His fingers drifted closer and closer to the ache between her legs. "Inequitable."

"A very good point," he agreed, pulling his cravat loose and dragging it across her torso. His shirt followed, billowing and landing next to her head.

She had been taught it was not polite to stare, but Thaxton would have to forgive her. The viscount in only his trousers was a sight to behold. If fencing was the exercise he got, it was more than enough to define his lean frame.

"You have not answered me," he said, easing her legs apart.

"Jonathan, you are in my bed. Is that not enough of an answer?"

"I would like to hear it all the same." He knelt at her feet, backlit by the dying fire at the hearth. His shadowed face looked amused. "As I am about to do something startlingly intimate, your explicit consent would very much reassure me."

She had no words as he leaned down, shimmying the chemise up to kiss her stomach. He pulled down her drawers, whisking them off her legs. She fought the urge to push him away, a strange, embarrassed instinct. She wanted him so much, but she had no idea what she wanted, just a nebulous sense of clinical terms. His tongue on her hip was not clinical, not at all. It was sublime. She stifled an undignified yelp.

"Say you are mine, Cassandra," he said, looking up from her torso. "Marry me."

"Yes," she breathed. "Yes, please keep . . ."

She did not know what she wanted him to continue doing, really. She could not find the thread of that sentence before it was obliterated by his kiss, in a place where she had never even been touched. She gasped and her head lolled back with the impossibly pleasurable sensation—she had not even known such a thing was involved in lovemaking. If it felt this good, why had no one mentioned it before? She sank into the bed like a limp poppet, her bare legs flanking the viscount, only his hair visible because his face was buried between her legs. Whatever magic he was doing with his tongue, she hoped he would never stop.

But he did.

"No," she pleaded, nearly a sob. "More."

He scaled her, his fingers finding her lips, pressing into them to silence her. He bit her ear, speaking softly into it.

"Yes, darling, but you are moaning. We want to be discovered, but not too soon. Moreover, those noises will make me lose all control."

"I think I am drunk," she whispered.

Thaxton smiled and lifted her chemise over her head. His eyes devoured her and his hands followed, his obvious lust squelching her impulse to cover herself.

"Thirteenth Countess Vane," he said with reverence. "I did not think you existed. Imagine my delight to find you are real."

His fingers traveled back to retrace the paths his tongue had laid, and she sighed in ecstasy. No feeling before came close to the euphoria of being touched by him. She just *wanted*—a building need that did not know where to attach. She tried to voice it, but he sank down again and then she could not think at all. He slipped a finger inside of her, and his tongue started working in concert with it. Her hand shot out to the side, grabbing a pillow to stifle the sounds that were spilling from her. She whimpered, shivered uncontrollably, and her thighs pressed in on his head.

She thought he said yes, and the thought of it made her shudder, hard, temporarily blinded by pleasure, as if the world were blotted out. She could not form a thought; she could not breathe. Would it go on forever? Was she mad? The pillow fell to her side, and she gasped in air, dizzy. Thaxton sat back on his knees, releasing a long breath. He mumbled something she couldn't hear.

"What did you say?"

"I said that you have an aptitude which I cannot wait to cultivate. For climax, that is."

"That was," she gasped, "highly improper."

"As a rule, I do not believe we should worry about propriety."

"No one told me about . . ." She searched for a word to define what had happened to her and was left wanting. "Climax" did not seem strong enough. There was not a word to describe it at all. Her whole body felt limp, sated, and weightless.

". . . that," she finished.

He smiled, his hands busy discarding his trousers, then his undergarments, in a flurry of fabric. Again, Cassandra fought and lost the battle to not stare. She had never seen a man completely naked, except for drawings and statues, which had not prepared her for what was in front of her.

Thaxton hovered over her, brushing her hair away from her neck and breasts, where it had curled, damp. He bit his lip, looking unaware that he had done it, a little unmoored. She could have sworn she saw love in his eyes—or she could imagine it was love at that moment.

"Your beauty turns my logical side inside out," he said, drawing in a deep breath. "I feel that I should tell you—once we . . . start . . . I may not be able to control myself for long. I have been thinking about this since we met."

He positioned himself on top of her, kissing her neck until she relaxed again, her arms curling around his strong back. She traced the muscles there, tense with need, and felt the tip of him press into her. She groaned, wishing he would just do it, hoping that it did not hurt as much as some of the ladies said. The ache in her had reached a crescendo, and he had to alleviate it.

"I need you," he said as a plea, his hands reaching behind her, gripping her buttocks and adjusting her hips. She stretched to accommodate him. It did not hurt, exactly, but she squirmed against him.

"Cassandra," he groaned, "I fear I cannot be gentle."

She moved her hips forward, pushing him in more.

"So," she whispered, "do not be gentle."

He definitely cursed that time, low and on a growl. Despite her permission and his need, he stayed steady and slow as he slid into her, and she bit her lip through the last of the pain.

He looked down, brushing a piece of hair from her face.

"I am yours," he said.

Chapter Nine

Thaxton awoke before Cassandra, and he gingerly extracted himself from their embrace, trying not to wake her in the process. Sometime in the middle of the night, they had become completely entwined. He pulled on his trousers, trying to compose the delicate note he had to send. *Dear Countess, Miss Seton is rightly ruined; please do come and be scandalized. Sincerely, Lord Thaxton.* In the end, he went with *Lady S— As we discussed, we would like to enlist your help. C's bedroom.* When he handed it to Sutton, in not much more than shirtsleeves, he received a look of censure so severe it made him glad he was barefoot—he had no boots in which to quake.

All he was concerned with was getting back to Cassandra's bed.

He closed the door on his return, trying not to wake her. He shed his shirt but kept on his trousers, sliding back into bed behind her. She stirred, her hair half hiding an angelic smile.

"Good morning, my lord. Are you ready to play the rogue?"

"Always." He smiled, burrowing in her neck.

"Lady Dorset will be furious."

"So will Miles. I am sure it will be great fun. Do you want to run away, or stay and watch the fireworks?"

"Maybe we should leave immediately. Honestly, Jonathan, we should have discussed this more. What if your father objects?"

"If he made any formal objection, no one would take him seriously. Besides, he is sentimental. All I will have to do is tell him I love you."

"You . . ."

Her sentence was left unfinished due to a knock at the door. Eliza had not taken long at all, Thaxton thought. Cassandra's eyes widened at the sound, though she had been well prepared for the moment. They had discussed it, in whispers, before they had fallen asleep.

"Don't worry," he murmured, extracting his body from the embrace. "Everything is arranged."

He opened the door with an exaggerated flourish, facing Cassandra, thinking it would be vastly amusing.

"Oh, my!" he exclaimed. "We are caught unawares. I shall have to marry you, Miss Seton."

"Over my dead body," Miles said from behind him.

Thaxton dimly heard Cassandra swear in a most unladylike fashion, clutching the covers at her throat.

"This is interesting," Miles continued, crossing into the room. "I suppose I should be hurt or surprised. I am neither."

"Anything but surprised," Thaxton quipped, as he always did when he did not know what his next move should be. He had hoped to have Cassandra in a carriage headed to the Vane estate well before Miles could cause a nasty scene. He buttoned his shirt hastily, adding his waistcoat, stalling.

"I will never cede her to you," Miles said, his self-possession colder than his rage ever had been. "I could not give a fig if she is ruined. Her money will spend."

"Would you care to talk in the hallway," Thaxton ground out, "while the lady makes herself decent?"

"Gladly," Miles said, brushing past him and out the door.

"Thax," Cassandra hissed from behind her wall of coverlet, "what the hell are you doing?"

"Reasoning with a beast. Get dressed."

"Do not let him goad you," she said. "He is deliberately goading you and has been all this time."

"It is not new to me," he muttered. "I can handle Markwick. Clothes, Cassie."

She shot him a glare, and he shut the door. She would have to forgive him later, he thought. He was surprised, angry, too on edge to watch his words.

"Nice try," Miles said without looking up from the breakfast tray he was marauding, which had been meant for Cassandra. "Very nice try, but foolish. Do you think I care that you sullied her? She may as well be a bag of money, not a woman. Did you think I would let you leave this house with her?"

"Frankly, I had not intended you would know until it was well past done."

Miles wiped his mouth with a napkin and discarded it on the tray.

"Always underestimating me," he said. "I shall be sure to remember that on my honeymoon when I am filling the love of your life with my heir."

"I should cut your tongue out," Thaxton said.

"Please keep saying things like that." Miles widened his eyes mockingly. "It goes *such* a long way in painting you as dangerously psychopathic."

Thaxton curled his itchy right fist. He was running out of reasons to not knock the man out and throw him in a carriage bound for the farthest reaches.

"I know you think are entitled to everything," Miles continued, "but you are not entitled to her. I am. She was promised to me before you ever met her. You may have your title, your power—what little there is left of that—and your wealth, but you will never have her."

The smug smile would be Miles's doom, Thaxton thought.

"And I will make each one of her days a living hell."

"Lucy left you," Thaxton surmised. "That changes your game, doesn't it?"

"My game, sir? I have no idea what you refer to. Your mad mind invented some affair between the medium and I. You have no proof."

Thaxton fell silent, thinking of the cuff links in his drawer. Fairly conclusive proof. Miles pounded on the door.

"Cassandra!" he yelled. "Do not dawdle."

"I understand your hurry," Thaxton drawled, "but there is no need to shout."

Miles whirled back to him.

"Be as droll as you want. We are leaving. You can no longer protect that"—he sputtered, his countenance getting redder and redder—"that whore."

Thaxton was rather pleased with the crack that rang out when he backhanded Miles, doubly pleased with the way Miles's head snapped sideways.

"Pistols," he heard himself say. "Dawn."

His ears rang, a metallic taste filled his mouth.

"You would not dare," Miles said, holding his cheek.

"You said over your dead body," Thaxton said. "So be it."

"So be it," Miles parroted, yanking off his glove and throwing it at Thaxton's feet. "I have been waiting for a reason to kill you."

Thaxton stared down at the glove. He had challenged Markwick to a duel of honor. And he had accepted.

Cassandra's fury would know no bounds.

"Lord Thaxton," the countess said, rounding the corner without knowing what she was getting into the middle of, "you are . . . dressed. And Markwick. Well, I . . ."

"Name your second," Miles seethed, not acknowledging Eliza.

Thaxton nodded to the countess.

"Good morning. Pardon me for a moment." He turned back to Miles, his eyes deepening to an angry blue-black. "Spencer is my second. He will agree. Take your time naming yours, if you can find anyone to stand on your honor. We will convene in twenty minutes to go over the rules."

Miles said nothing more, but his glare said volumes. He stormed away, and Thaxton hastily ushered Eliza into the bedroom, shutting and locking the door behind them. He felt as if he was panting, and he leaned against the back of the door, closing his eyes for a moment.

"I must assume something went wrong," Eliza said. "Why was Miles here?"

"He burst in," Cassandra explained. She was mostly dressed, but her hair could have used the attention of a calm hand. "We thought he was you, actually."

Thaxton's mouth would not open to tell them what had transpired in the hall. He knew he should. He also knew what the reaction would be. If he sank back any farther into the door, he would become a part of it.

"Jonathan?" Cassandra asked. "Are you quite all right?"

"*Erm.* He—he still wants to marry you."

She crossed to his side, her tone still light but now cautious.

"I suppose we shall have to make a scene, then."

He closed his eyes.

"Cassandra, I challenged Miles to a duel. I am sorry." He took a breath.

She coughed. "I must have heard you wrong."

"No, I most certainly told him pistols at dawn. He dishonored you, and he has been assassinating my character for as long as I have had one," he said, the gravity of the situation settling in his stomach. "I will have satisfaction for his crimes, by the gentlemen's code of honor. It is the only option left for resolving this feud. I am only surprised it had not happened sooner."

"But no one duels anymore," Cassandra said, stunned. "You must be joking."

"Slow down, what?" Eliza said.

"Sometime soon, at dawn, Miles and I will pace ten apart and turn pistols on each other. I do not know how to make it any clearer. He called Cassandra . . . a dreadful slur, I will not repeat it . . . but to be honest, I should have slapped him a thousand times before then."

The rest of his explanation was lost to the flurry of Cassandra's balled-up fists, fluttering against his chest.

"You fool! You idiot!"

Cassandra thought she must be screaming. She hoped she was screaming. He deserved it. She pummeled Thaxton with fists and words at the same time, though both barely connected in her frenzy of angry panic.

"You *idiot*. How could you—why would you? Miles could do anything—tell my stepmother, use it to force the issue, or worse, go through with the duel. He will kill you—he *wants* to kill you! You lost your temper and now, now, now—"

He seized her wrists, stilling her.

"He will not kill me."

"This cannot happen in my house," Eliza said from directly behind Cassandra. She could hear the tremor in her friend's voice, not see it.

"It will be outside, Countess," Thaxton said.

"Do not," Cassandra growled, hitting him on the chest with each word, "be-glib-right-now!"

"Pardon. Defensive glibness. But I am afraid that this is not a woman's matter, and I do not expect either of you to understand. I cannot back down from something like this."

"Dueling is illegal," Cassandra said, trying another tack.

"As is prostitution, but that does not seem to stop anyone."

"And barbaric."

"Miles's conduct has been barbaric. And this is the end result of that."

He seemed so composed, as if he had not just altered his fate wholly. Her thoughts were racing, even as her hands stilled. The number of ways in which this duel of supposed honor could go wrong was so astronomical, she could not begin to process it.

"I should get Spencer," Eliza said. "He will put a stop to this."

"Yes, please do," Thaxton said. "I need to speak with him, but I would also appreciate a moment alone with Cassandra."

The request seemed all the more absurd because she had not moved, fists balled up on his lapels.

"I imagine you two have things you need to discuss," Eliza said, nodding her head. "I will be back directly."

As soon as the countess exited, Thaxton removed Cassandra's hands from his chest and pulled her to him. She did not resist—she felt boneless, she could not. She burrowed her head into him, her voice stifled by his velvet jacket.

"You are going to leave me."

"No, never, my love," he said, stroking her hair. "I am going to shoot that bastard; then you and I are going to elope to Gretna Green. It will all be very dramatic, which I think is fitting, no?"

She realized she was crying. His collar had gone damp.

"This is daft," she said.

"Again, fitting."

Cassandra fought the urge to call him an idiot again. She looked down at her hand—sometime in the middle of the night, he had slipped his mother's ring onto her finger. It fit perfectly.

"Do not do it," she said. "Back out."

"Miles is a terrible shot. He cannot hit the broad side of a boat. I am not in any real danger."

"Do not do this," she repeated, thinking she could somehow hammer it into his brain. That each repetition would build upon the previous until he came to his senses.

"Impossible. The man deserves at the very least one bullet for his transgressions."

"But there is so much we do not know. What was his plan with the séance? Why would he do that to you? He does not stand to inherit your estate. He had no motivation other than disliking you."

"Hating me."

"Hating you. He will shoot too soon."

"He is far too concerned with reputation to do that. Too many witnesses."

"This is incredibly rash," she said, at wits' end. "You are not thinking. At all."

"More polite way of calling me a fool, but the sentiment is the same. I do not disagree with you. I would take it back if I could, Cassie, but understand, the wheels in motion now cannot be stopped."

Eliza returned on Spencer's heels, which may as well have been ablaze. He stalked into the room in an opera of fury, pushing Thaxton hard enough to dislodge him from Cassandra. She stumbled before managing to step out of the way of Spencer's momentum.

"You. Bloody. Fool."

Thaxton shrank back as Spencer advanced.

"Congratulate me, Spence. I am to be married."

"Damn right you are." He kept walking, forcing Thaxton back farther. "What were you thinking—in Cassandra's room of all places? Did you *want* Markwick to find you? Did you want to challenge him?"

"I do not think he did," Cassandra said.

"I did not ask you, Miss Seton. Jonathan, explain to me what is going on, in plain terms, without your characteristic verbal flourishes."

"Cassandra and I got carried away last night. Before we could arrange something more discreet, Miles stormed in. I do not know why he would be here, except to try to catch us at what he indeed caught us at. He needled me, insisting that he will not break the engagement. And worse. I snapped."

"Staggering. Reckless." Spencer turned his back on Thaxton and walked again to the ladies. "Disappointing. Thaxton, you will be in my study in one hour. Miss Seton, your mother will be waiting at breakfast—it would behoove all of us to act like this is a normal morning."

"You are allowing this to happen?" Eliza said, incredulous.

"The moment Thaxton spoke the words, it was done," Spencer said firmly. "You will not understand—nor do I expect you to. It is a ridiculous way to resolve things."

Thaxton was looking at the floor. Cassandra wanted to squeeze his hand, something, to reassure him, but she stopped herself shy of moving.

"No one can know about this," he said, not looking up. "Above all, Lady Dorset cannot find out. Only the people here and whomever Miles chooses as his second. Spencer, please speak with him as soon as you can about secrecy. And during the duel, it will be just the four men."

"I will be on that field no matter what you decree," Cassandra huffed.

"You absolutely will not. We can discuss this later," he answered tightly. "When we are calmer."

"Calmer?" Cassandra winced at the raise of her voice. "I am calm."

She had never been less so.

The man she loved, whom she had just lost her virginity to, did not care about his life. He never had—the duel was the final proof of it. From the alcohol to the isolation, he was looking for something to kill him. Cassandra suspected that Miles would be happy to grant that wish.

Thaxton had always tried to choose death over life. She had done nothing to change that.

When she emerged from that wretched epiphany, Spencer and Eliza had vacated the room. Cassandra did not know if they had said goodbye, or how much conversation she had missed. Thaxton was regarding her with a worried brow.

"Please try to understand," he said, drawing her back to him. She felt limp in his arms, but so far from the limp satisfaction she had felt the night before. "And forgive me. Next week, this will all be a memory."

"Yes, but will you be here to share it?"

"Cassie, please. Do not quarrel with me. I cannot bear it."

"I have to go to breakfast now," she said, carefully picking up his arms and laying them at his sides. "I am sure you should get ready for your very important meeting in the earl's study."

"Please do not shut me out." Thaxton frowned. "Can you . . . see me later?"

"Later," she said, turning before she had to endure another moment looking at his face, which was both sad and hopeful.

She found she would much prefer remorse.

She heard him walk out. Cassandra fumed as she began to change, with the help of a concerned-looking but suspiciously silent lady's maid. Go to breakfast indeed, with all this on her mind. Of course she would fall in love with a man bent on throwing himself into the abyss—of course. She had no luck to speak of, as far as love went. She slipped off the sapphire ring that she supposed was an engagement ring—a ruination ring—and returned it to the chain around her neck. No need to invite questions she could not answer.

Eliza joined her shortly, sitting on her bed. Her friend could not hide her concern, hovering as if she expected Cassandra to do something drastic. Yet before they could begin any sort of conversation, Lady Dorset stormed in.

"Where have you been all morning, Cassandra?"

Both women froze, unsure of how to answer, terrified that she knew.

"I see," Lady Dorset said. "Your silence tells me my intuition is right." She turned her eyes to Eliza. "Madam, your household is not under your control."

"I beg your pardon," Eliza said, standing. "I have done nothing but provide for your every comfort."

"Do you think I would not notice my ward, gone for hours at a time, sneaking around, likely with that lunatic?"

To Eliza's credit, she did not blink.

"Cassie is not your ward, my lady. She is the marquess's daughter. And though it is none of your concern, you can be assured that if you think she is missing, she is merely with me. There are many things to be done, and her company is appreciated."

Lady Dorset scowled.

"Very well. I shall see if Mr. Markwick agrees with your excuses."

"I am sure he will," Cassandra said.

The marchioness flounced out without saying good-bye.

"And a good afternoon to you, Lady Dorset," Eliza called.

When they were alone, Eliza sighed and sank into a wicker chair.

"I will never do this again," she said. "It is misery."

"Spencer's family is pleased, so you can rest assured they approve of you." Cassandra smiled. "I knew you would be a wonderful countess."

"So will you."

She had not thought about it, but it was true. If all went according to the tenuous and ill-conceived plan, she would be the Countess Vane, wife of the Ghost, London's most reviled bachelor. If he survived the duel, that was. *If.*

"Oh, Eliza. Why would he do this?"

"His temper was frayed. And Miles does nothing but nettle him—I see now that you were correct."

"Not that it matters, at this point."

A scowl crossed Eliza's face, which Cassandra found all the more jarring on her sunny friend.

"I did not like the way both Spencer and Thaxton barred us from the field. They think they can keep us out of this."

"They cannot. We need a plan. We are good at plans," Cassandra said, trying for optimism, though she felt fairly hopeless.

"First of all, we need a spy," Eliza said, revealing that she had already been thinking about it. "I will speak with Sutton—he will disapprove of the whole thing and be willing to turn coat on Thaxton's privacy. Deeply unethical, though."

"And a duel is not?"

"Complicated question. But it is clear that low tactics are required. I will speak with Sutton, but I think we should pin down the rest later—forgive me, Cassandra, but you look very tired."

"You are right," she sighed. "Exhausted."

Eliza hugged her tightly; then they parted.

Cassandra spent the rest of the day in bed, unable to sleep and paralyzed with fear.

❧

Other than a brief stop to change, Thaxton went straight to Spencer's study. He sat in the corner, inert as he had ever been. Without a fire, the study became tomblike and damp. Since the morning, he had been wondering why the hell he had challenged Miles. It had just . . . come out of him. Unbidden. He wanted to think it was unbidden, but Cassandra had made it so he was analyzing his every motivation. How could he have done something so harebrained as to issue a duel challenge? He was the happiest he had ever been, so why would he do that? The first painful thorns of optimism were poking into his heart, but his own actions had done their best to crush them.

"Do you always put yourself in the spookiest place on purpose?" Spencer said, approaching his desk. "I did not even see you at first."

"I suppose I do," Thaxton said, still contemplative. "Though I do not think I was conscious of it until now."

"Perhaps you have been unconscious for a long time?"

"Perhaps," he said in a small voice, not one he would normally use around Spencer. It sounded weak. He glanced at Spencer, trying to gauge his feelings, and spied Sutton in the corner. The valet had not even said hello, but stood stalwart. Spencer did not mention or otherwise explain his presence, so Thaxton imagined he had asked the servant to be there.

"In the interest of time, let us assume that you are well aware of how stupid this was, no matter how much Miles pushed you. So I can save you the lecture about your utter foolishness."

"Your unspoken lecture is ringing in my ears. I agree, by the way." Thaxton paused, feeling a rush of embarrassing sentimentality. "Thank you for being my second, Spence."

"There is no question of that. I am willing to stand on your honor. Always. If you had asked me to stand up for your sense, however . . ."

Thaxton waved a hand. "Enough, enough, I take the point."

The door opened, and Miles strode in, looking more confident than Thaxton would have liked. He tossed a frown at the corner where Thaxton lurked, then bowed his head to Spencer.

"My lord," he said in his sniveling voice, "I am sorry it has come to this."

"Are you?" Spencer demanded, showing far more emotion than the second to a duelist should. Tradition would have him remain impassive, but the earl seemed to disagree with that rule. "Are you really, Markwick?"

"Do you think I want to duel with this deranged maniac?" Miles's eyes were black. He gestured to the corner like a child on the verge of a tantrum.

"Then apologize," Thaxton said, not making any effort to come out of the shadows or dignify Miles's presence by standing. "And cede."

"Never. I spoke the truth."

"Not once in your life, have you."

"Dog," Miles hissed.

"You should be calling me either my lord or Lord Thaxton, I do not hesitate to remind you."

"I shan't call you anything, then."

"Enough," Spencer said, rubbing his temple. "If neither of you will back down, then there are formalities we must discuss. Time, location, pistols, and Markwick's second. I will need to speak with the man."

"There is no one here at the moment. I am trying to find a delicate way to approach it."

"Think fast," Thaxton said. "I have my pistols, Spencer. No need to dredge yours out."

"You carry your dueling pistols?" Miles asked.

"Listen to yourself, Thaxton," Spencer sighed. "I sometimes think you want people to believe you insane."

"It paid off to carry the pistols. One never knows. And now I am merely the most prepared man."

"I have no complaints," Miles said. "It will expedite the process, in fact. And I am perfectly willing to kill you with your own pistol."

"It is refreshing that your threats are so overt now," Thaxton said. "I wish you would have done so earlier. If you are feeling honest, I have a few pertinent questions."

"Address them on the field," Miles bit off.

"Gladly."

"So much bravado," Spencer sighed. "And so little reason for it. Both of you."

"The west lawn," Thaxton said decisively, impatient with the arguing. "On the other side of the pawn. Daybreak, not tomorrow, but the day after."

"Agreed," Miles said.

"For once," Spencer added.

Miles bowed. "If there's nothing further, I would like to pay a visit to my fiancée. We have much to discuss."

"The hell you will," Thaxton flared.

"Neither of you should see Miss Seton until dinner. As it stands, we need to act like everything is normal. Everything must proceed as if Cassandra and Miles are to be married."

"That is the best course," Miles said, satisfied. "I will inform you when my second arrives so that you may arrange a meeting, but I doubt any agreement can be reached. The duel will happen. Is that all, my lord?"

Spencer waved an irritated hand. "Get out."

Miles obliged, leaving without so much as a farewell.

"I am going to see her, you know," Thaxton said.

"I know."

"I gave her my mother's ring, and she gave me a yes. After the duel, and if she agrees, we will go straight to Scotland and elope. Damn the scandal—society does not want me anyway."

"I do not believe you should make any more hasty decisions. And Miles was right about one thing—you need to set your affairs in order. See Miss Seton in the evening, but write letters now. I do not think you will die at the end of Markwick's gun, but since you are willing to perish for your honor, you ought to put it into practice."

Four hours later, Thaxton had a stack of five sealed letters, addressed, top to bottom, to his secretary, his solicitor, Spencer, his father, and Cassandra. He had written them in order of least to most painful. He hoped they would never be opened. It gave him more reason to survive the duel—he did not want the seals cracked. They all held an embarrassing amount of emotion.

He considered skipping dinner but needed to see Cassandra's face.

She was keeping up the pretense of being Markwick's fiancée, it seemed. He could understand why, but it burned. If there was even a chance that he had just a few days left on earth, he would want to spend them in any other way than watching Cassandra sit silently next to that cur. Just before dinner, in the parlor, she had touched his arm and whispered, "This is torture." And it was, indeed. It was nearly impossible to act as if nothing was going on, between the duel and the sentiments he could no longer seem to contain.

A funny thing had happened after writing those letters. He found that in imagining his death, he desperately wanted to live. So he wrote one more note, for immediate delivery to Cassandra:

Portrait Hall, Very Urgent. Yours, J.

⁓❦⁓

Cassandra paced the portrait hall in a state of high agitation. She could not believe that they had not called it off yet. She had been waiting all day to hear that someone, anyone, had come to his senses. Spencer, Thaxton, Miles: it did not matter which one, just that one of them had stopped the farce. It had apparently been too much to think that even one in three men would behave logically.

Sutton had thankfully been able to get quite a lot of information on the duel by showing up to the meeting between the opponents. Eliza said the valet had been rather proud of himself: he had not asked to be invited, but they had never once questioned his presence. Thanks to that blessing, they had the date and time of the duel. That day, both Cassandra and Eliza would be on the field.

She turned around midpace to find Thaxton standing next to a portrait of Spencer's severe grandfather.

"I love you," he said before she could even get out a greeting. "I fear I had not made it abundantly clear, but I love you, Cassandra. That is why I want to marry you, and all other reasons are incidental."

Everything she had been meaning to say flew from her mind. Her voice came out far more quiet and unsure than she had intended.

"Well, I love you, too." Cassandra fumbled for all of the speeches she had planned, the cutting remarks, the reasonable rationale contriving to bring him round. She found nothing. Just the simple truth. "But I fail to understand why you cannot take it back. And if you say it is an exclusively male activity, I will strangle you."

"Then I must give you my throat."

"We should leave, Jonathan." She came forward to clasp his hands, feeling very at sea. She had the distinct feeling that nothing she could say would change the situation. "We should leave tonight."

"I cannot. Markwick would come after us, and I would be humiliated. I know society thinks I am daft, but I would rather they not think me a coward, too."

"It is a consistent worry of mine how little you value your life," she said.

He did not answer, and it made the portrait room too soundless, like an unused church. As if the air had gone stale. He had worn gray—why had he done that? His eyes matched the fabric, and it rendered his whole form drawn and sad. Ashen. Half in and half out of this world. Like an apparition.

She had fallen in love with a ghost. She should have known. Society had been right, but not in the superficial definition they were employing. Thaxton was a ghost, but it was not because he was absent, but because he had never been fully alive.

"I know you could not wear the ring at dinner," he said, tentative, "but I hope that does not mean . . ."

She yanked the chain out of her bodice, cutting off his sentence. She felt so angry, so unable to reconcile his love for her and his willingness to throw himself into the arms of the grim reaper.

"I am not leaving you, Jonathan, but I should. All this time, you have been telling me you are destined to be mad—I never believed it until today."

"Fair enough," he said quietly. "Fair enough."

The gilt portraits flanked him, pressed in on him. Or she was imagining things. He seemed surrounded, suffocated. Cassandra wished they were anywhere but among the rows of nobles' eyes, oppressive and judgmental. And Thaxton had been the one who had chosen this room. Rows and rows of men sitting, men standing, in court dress, with hunting hounds. Women who were either dour or ethereal, with no in-between. Families, unhappy families. Stretching generations back, hanging on to their histories and honor and rot.

"You cannot expect me to stand idly by while this happens," she said. "Do what you have to do, and so will I. For now, we both need rest."

"Am I being dismissed?" Thaxton sounded as if he could not decide whether he was offended or amused.

"Yes," she said. "Think on your sins."

She knew she was being harsh, that she should have spent have more time talking to him or even spent the night. But if he was so convinced that he was not going to die, then what need she worry about time? She could not help but simmer in anger. He did not even realize that the hotheadedness of the duel was leaving her to investigate on her own.

Which was why she was going straight to Lucy Macallister's chambers.

Not a single candle burned in the hallway; they expected no one to visit Lucy. It was not lost on Cassandra that the last time she had been to the room was to rifle through the woman's personal belongings. Shortly before exposing her as a fraud in front of a phalanx of nobility.

Come to think of it, Cassandra could not imagine she would be a welcome guest. She ventured to knock gently on the door.

"Come in," Lucy's voice, hoarse, said from behind it.

Cassandra turned the knob with a creak. Inside, the room was inky, with a sheen of moonlight emanating from the sheer white curtains. Lucy had the covers pulled up to her neck, ensconced in the large canopy bed, the same model in each lower guest room. Her kimono lay draped over a lamp, casting reds and oranges through the light.

"It is Cassandra," she said, tentative. "I come in peace."

"Peace?" Lucy sounded cynical. "It is too late for that."

As Cassandra drew closer, she could make out Lucy's puffy eyes and drawn face. She had been crying, probably for hours. A sharp stab of guilt went through her. This looked for all the world like a grieving woman, not a calculating schemer bent on taking down anyone. How could she have not seen it before?

"I am sorry," she said slowly, weighing her words, "about what happened at the last séance. It was badly done of me."

"I deserved it," Lucy said.

"Not . . . the way I did it." Cassandra crossed to the side of the bed, gesturing to a chair. "May I sit?"

Lucy nodded.

"Are you ill?" Cassandra studied her. "Eliza said you were not feeling well."

"Never felt worse, actually." Lucy averted her eyes, staring at the curtain. The window, open a crack, rustled the material. "Though I do not see why you should care."

"I do not hate you, Lucy. I was hoping we might talk frankly."

"A forthright talk between us may be fraught with danger, Miss Seton."

"No, I know you hate formality. Cassie. Please."

"Cassie," Lucy repeated. "I am afraid I have been operating under the wrong impression of you."

"I think I may be guilty of the same."

The silence between them felt like a gap closing.

"I wanted to hate you," Lucy said, "because I love Miles. I know you do not care about him, but I do—I did. I thought he was also sincere in that affection."

"I know nothing of Miles's mind. I do not know him." Cassandra paused, her eyes drawn to the window where low fog crept over the hills. "I am going to marry Lord Thaxton. You and I have no quarrel."

"Not over men." Lucy pulled herself up in bed, straightening her back against the multitude of pillows. "What I do—mediumship—is not the fraud you think it is."

"I understand it is somehow important to you, but why then use it in the way that you have?"

"I cannot . . . I cannot possibly explain to you why I did it. Miles seemed to think that . . . that we could be together. We fell in love slowly while he was in Scotland. I knew he was engaged, but he kept telling me he would find a way out of it. He kept asking worse and worse things of me, insisting he had a plan. It all seemed different before I knew any of you; Miles painted Thaxton as a man who deserved to have his fortune taken away. And if he had Thaxton's fortune, then we could marry and he would still be able to finish the Scottish estate, elite stables, and everything. There is no reason I should have done what I did, except that I was in love and it drove me a little mad." There were tears in her voice. "I am so very sorry."

"I know that feeling," Cassandra said. "Love driving one mad, I mean."

"My mediumship started out separate from what I had with Miles, but it got tangled with it." Lucy reached for the glass of tea on her nightstand, which had to be cold. She drank it anyway. "Please do not think I am insincere in my beliefs. I lied to Thaxton for Miles, but it is not something I have ever done or would ever do again. I disgraced my gift and disrespected all of you. I wish I could take it all back."

"Lucy, there is something I must tell you. Thaxton challenged Miles to a duel, which will be in one day's time. This has gone far beyond whatever it was conceived to accomplish."

"A duel?"

"Yes, I know. Let it sink in for a moment."

"We certainly cannot let them do that."

Cassandra smiled in the darkness. "I am so glad you said that."

Chapter Ten

Thaxton slept sitting up that night, outside of Cassandra's door and around the corner, for fear that Markwick would try to do something terrible.

He saw her return to her room from wherever she had been. He wanted Cassandra's forgiveness, craved it, but knew he did not deserve it. It would be wrong to press her for it. But he also did not believe she was entirely safe.

So, he slept against a wall, his topcoat propped under him to ease the pressure. No one passed in the evening, or if they did, they did not make an effort to rouse him. Thaxton had never been a heavy sleeper, so he was fairly certain that once he heard the morning maid enter Cassandra's room, it had been a quiet night. He stretched and returned to his room.

The early hour of the morning made him think of the next. Hopefully, the carriage carrying Miles's second would arrive that evening, and they could have a quick meeting that would seal the event. All the waiting was bad for his nerves. He had no idea what to do with himself, and little will to socialize. Since his reputation preceded him there, he did not think he would be missed if he eschewed all responsibilities and supervised the packing of his trunks.

He wanted to be ready to leave as soon as the smoke cleared on the shots that finally cowed Miles. He was hoping that the blackguard would be more forthcoming when a few bullets had narrowly missed him. Any duel Thaxton had heard about (and he had been to two himself) rarely resulted in death. It was mostly quite a bit of yelling, gunplay more to wound or scare than kill, and an awful lot of noise. Deaths in duels were discouraged.

But Cassandra was right. There was no counting on Miles playing by the rules. In fact, there was precedent that he would not. It was time to think about preparations in advance of that. He knew he could count on the pistols not being tampered with, since they would be using his set. There was nothing to be done about the possibility that Miles would shoot to kill, but Thaxton did not think that would happen.

Miles wanted acceptance, not infamy.

A knock came at his door, a superfluous knock, because Spencer entered well before he could be given leave.

"I am about to tell you something, but first I need you to promise me that you will remain calm."

"Not a good start. Go on."

"Your promise, Thax."

"I promise, Spence, go on."

"Your father is here."

Thaxton's feet were moving before he even knew where he was going. Why would his father be here? *How* would his father be here? Spencer followed behind him, now in full rant.

"I am standing on your honor tomorrow, Thaxton. Do not panic, do not yell, do not scare him. He seems fine to the outward perception. This is not the end of the world."

Thaxton whirled.

"Is it not? Percy, my father has not been in a room with more than three people for years. He very well cannot be here."

"He knew who I was, Jonathan, so he is fine at the moment. His eyes look bright and he is mostly lucid, even if he wanders in conversation." Spencer paused. "Give it a chance. It is worse that he has been cooped up in the house all this time."

"It sounds suspiciously like you are questioning my judgment in the matter."

"I am."

The two men faced each other, the sound of their breathing the only noise for a moment. Sutton appeared at the end of the hallway.

"Let us assess the situation," Spencer said. "Come, talk to your father, but do not storm there."

Thaxton took a moment to think before rushing into the fray, which was something he barely ever did. It was time he cultivated thinking before raging. He realized he would not have even considered it in the past. He would have raged first and thought later. But after the reactionary duel challenge, Cassandra made her point well. She deserved better than a man who overreacted and made situations worse. It had also been a long time since he had been around his father while sober, so that might make a difference. He let his breathing return to normal before starting to walk downstairs.

"He showed up in his carriage with one servant," Spencer said. "He does not seem to know anything about the duel, said he just thought he might spend the last few days of the house party in 'the pleasant company.'"

Thaxton put a hand to his head, rubbing it over his eyes.

"What could have possessed him?"

"He mentioned a letter from Miles—saying that he was missed here and should join the party. The rat must have sent it even before the duel."

They descended the stairs in a clatter, Thaxton leading by merit of the fact that he was in a full panic, exactly what Spencer had warned against.

The Earl Vane stood at the bottom of the stairs.

"My son!" he said, coming halfway up the stairs to meet Thaxton, his hands at his cheeks. "I thought you were never coming home."

Thaxton shrank from his father's embrace, glimpsing his father's valet, their oldest family servant, behind him.

"Sykes," he said, as evenly as he could, "why was this allowed to happen?"

"Sorry, sir. He insisted he could travel," the valet said. "We ran out of reasons to put him off. Could not be helped."

"Jonathan, Jonathan." His father patted his cheek. "You look so well."

Thaxton backed up one stair, a little above his father. He could see the very top of his head, his wispy gray hair so thin that pink skin shown through it.

"Papa. I told you I would be back in a fortnight."

"It has been more than a fortnight."

"No, it has not; you are confused. I would have been home in three days."

"We should take this conversation to the parlor." Spencer put a hand at Thaxton's back and prodded both Vanes down the stairs. Some of the guests were finishing breakfast and throwing curious glances in their direction as they moved to their next destination. Sykes took hold of the elder earl and guided him along.

The morning light lent the air in the parlor a yellow haze. No one made any move to change that by drawing the curtains.

"Please, sit." Spencer gestured to the copse of seats in the corner. "I will have someone get tea."

It was good of him to try to normalize it.

"Papa," Thaxton said, sitting down across from his father, who had plopped down after looking all around the room, "I wish you would not have done this."

"Why do you get to go on holiday, but I do not?"

"You never asked." Thaxton knew he did not quite speak the truth. His father had not asked, but even if he had, Thaxton would not have let him go.

"The house went wonky while you were away. Walls are moving; do you think we should employ an architect? Your mother says it is not necessary, but I do not believe her. Will you find one? An architect?"

"Yes, Papa."

Thaxton had learned that it was best to agree with his father.

Spencer returned, followed shortly by a tea tray. The Earl Vane accepted a cup without incident and sipped, again looking all around the room. He seemed too serene. Thaxton had always thought that being in public would further unruffle him, but the opposite seemed true. He had even remembered Spencer.

"Tell me what you have been doing," the Earl Vane said, quite like a normal person. Thaxton fought to not be slack-jawed.

"He met a girl," Spencer answered, standing behind Thaxton's chair.

"You did?" The brightness of his father's eyes shocked Thaxton. The earl looked genuinely happy.

"I, er. I have."

"Capital," the elder Vane said. "Right age to meet a girl."

Thaxton raised a skeptical eyebrow.

"But you have always said I should not fall in love."

"You should not, but it is inevitable."

Spencer laughed.

"Wise words, sir. Come with me and we will get you settled in. You should stay for the rest of the house party and enjoy yourself; then you and Thaxton can return to London together."

"Thank you, Spencer. You are too kind."

Thaxton stood with his father, awash in confusion. Not only was he polite to others, but he also seemed able to hold conversations. Of course, he was not all there, but it was the best he had been in months.

What to do with that knowledge?

After further talk with Lucy, Cassandra and Eliza had a concrete plan. It felt good to have steps in place, even if the plot did not seem exactly foolproof. Revolving, as it did, around Lucy's last revelation, their trump card, and timing on the field, it could easily backfire, but it was more than they had at the beginning of the day.

It seemed strange that the rest of the house party went on as if nothing out of the ordinary was happening. At Cassandra's home, word traveled faster among the staff than the family.

If all was going well, Lucy was already started on her part of the plan. For now, Cassandra would take breakfast in her room. She was not sure if she wanted to see Thaxton or not—to see him and risk hearing that the duel was still a reality or that he had come to his senses and called it off. She settled for imagining the latter, how she would collapse into his arms, thank him, tell him that she loved him so.

That seemed unlikely, though.

Thaxton's voice followed a soft knock at her door. "Cassie. Quick. Let me in."

The remains of her breakfast lingered on a small table, and she eyed the door warily. There was a moment where she thought she should let him wait, but the urgency of his tone scared her. He entered as soon as she opened the door, hardly even a crack, and shut it tightly behind him.

"My father is here," he said on a breath. "My father is here."

She took both his hands in hers. "Calm down."

"Why would he come? Why would he come?"

"He is your father, Jonathan. Why are you so scared of him? He raised you from a young child. The man he was remains, just . . . buried." She paused, considering whether she should say the next thing on her tongue. She decided to go with yes. It was honest. "Have you considered, possibly, that your pushing him away has made the situation worse?"

"That is very close to what Spencer said," he replied with narrowed eyes.

"And have you noticed that if he and I agree, we are generally right?"

"That remains to be seen."

Cassandra frowned. "It is a distinct talent of yours to go from panicked to flippant."

"It is not a talent. It is a reaction."

She sat back down, exasperated. Anticipating his moods and vagaries exhausted her as the duel loomed. His willingness to follow fancy to his own detriment seemed so much easier to excuse before, but now it might get him killed.

"If you want to talk, Jonathan, sit down. If you want to trade witticisms, please go elsewhere."

He declined to sit.

"You do not intend on forgiving me, do you? About the duel, I mean. Even if I survive, I have broken . . . this. Us."

"I have not made a decision, truth be told."

"Then this would be the wrong time to ask if you would like to meet my father before dinner."

"The most wrong of times. Does he even know about the duel?"

"I hope he never will."

"Instead of trying to explain to him who I am, you should have a discussion about the threat to the life of his heir."

"He does not care about the line, if you recall."

"How could I forget, Thaxton? Please, sit if you are staying, and leave if you must. Your hovering is making me vastly nervous."

"I am going; I must attend to father. I simply want to know if you are mine or not. It matters a great deal to how I proceed."

"Am I yours? Listen to yourself. Are you mine?"

He actually took a step back.

"You would be the second person to tell me to listen to myself in two days. Would you like to guess who the first one was?"

Cassandra took a sip of her tea, which bought a moment of time.

"Please go attend to your father," she said steadily. "I will see you at dinner."

"But you will be with Miles."

"Yes. I will be with Miles. How else do you propose we do this? Tell the whole house party about my ruining and, inevitably, the duel?"

"A salient point." He bowed stiffly. "I will take my leave. If you would like to talk, I am sure I will have trouble sleeping tonight."

She nearly cracked then, he sounded so desolate. She knew she would go see him tonight, but until then, she did not want him to think he was forgiven. One did not just issue a duel and expect to get off scot-free. Instead, she watched his back as he turned away, watched him close the door, holding her breath so that she would not tell him to stay.

The parlor before the evening meal buzzed with guests talking about making plans to travel back home and what a nice getaway this had been. It seemed odd to Cassandra that these two weeks had felt like a lark to anyone.

They had been the most eventful of her life.

"Miss Seton," Miles said, approaching her and bowing, "thank you for making this simple."

"I fail to see any other choice I have in the matter." She lowered her voice, glancing around to make sure no one was paying attention. "Nor in the matter of our marriage. I am ruined, and I shall marry my ruiner. So, you see, I would rather you not kill him."

"I have no intention of killing him. I intend to wound him, maybe beyond recognition, depending on how well he keeps his mouth shut during the rounds. And if you will recall, I did not issue the challenge. I found him in your room, yet I kept my head." He paused, holding out his arm for the dinner procession. "Let the record state Lord Thaxton has never kept his head."

Cassandra could not help craning her neck to see if she could glimpse the Earl Vane. Would the mysterious father that she had heard so much about come down to dinner? Was he well enough to do so? Did he look like his son? Did he know anything of the intrigue that had been going on while Thaxton was away from home? These were all things Cassandra should have asked when Thaxton was in her room earlier, but it would have burst a hole in her deliberate unapproachability, which was already on tenuous ground. The procession line wrapped around a corner, and she could not see either Vane.

Eliza had broken the party up further for the last formal dinner. Four tables of ten lined the wide, high-ceilinged room, lit with oil lamps. The guest ranks had thinned now that the house party neared its end, and the countess had chosen tables to mix up the conversation and protect the people who kept the secret of the duel. The setup caused a bit of a jumble in the dining room proper, everyone looking around to find assigned spots, marked by little cards in front of each setting. Miles went to say hello to Lady Beatrice and her mother, leaving Cassandra to find their settings.

Of course, she bumped clumsily into Thaxton between two tables.

"Sorry," he said, lowering his gaze. "God, you look beautiful. Sorry. I am trying to act as if nothing is going on, I swear. Good evening, Miss Seton."

"Good evening, Lord Thaxton. No need to apologize." Cassandra looked down at the cards on the table next to her. She hoped it gave him a good view of her long neck, adorned with her best necklace to hide the smaller chain that held his ring. Her dress, a deep maroon crepe, looked fragile, as if it might tear under the right hands. She had known what she was doing when she put it on. "It looks as if I am here."

His gaze was locked on her when she looked back up, and she could see from the heat in his eyes that she had made the right decision. Let him think on that dress when he was meeting with the men about the duel. Thaxton picked up his card from the table, the chair across from Miles, next to her aunt Arabella. Cassandra could not help but notice that Lucy's name was nowhere to be seen; she must not have come down to dinner at all.

"And I am here," he said.

"Where is your father?" she asked, trying to sound optimistic, unaffected, and pleasant, though she was sure it did not work.

"Yonder, with the dowager." He indicated Spencer's mother, a small but sturdy woman in a giant gown, smiling on the arm of the man who must be the earl, judging from his resemblance to Thaxton. He peered back at the table. "They are seated here as well. I am sure they will be along any moment. For the record, he does not remember Lucy. Or he has forgotten her."

His father and Spencer's mother were still talking as they arrived at the table.

"You, Earl Vane, always kept a party lively," the dowager said with a smile. "I imagine that has not changed."

The earl laughed, eyes more alert than Cassandra thought they would be. He did not look half as bad as Thaxton prepared her for.

"Father," Thaxton said, now that they were all at their places, "I would like you to meet Miss Cassandra Seton, daughter of the Marquess of Dorset, though she prefers not to use the honorific."

The earl looked at her. She felt sure he would give her the usual reaction to an introduction like that—an amused look, patronizing, or outright chagrin. But he just smiled.

"I like a woman who knows her own mind. A pleasure to meet you, Miss Seton." The earl bowed his head, then turned back to the dowager with a smile.

"You have always known *your* own mind, Lady Spencer," he said, causing the dowager to giggle, not a sound you would expect out of the stately and somewhat dour woman.

The elders began reminiscing, and Thaxton smiled at Cassandra. "I think my father is flirting with Spencer's mother."

"You two should not be speaking," Miles said, arriving next to Cassandra. He pulled out her chair, or rather he yanked it out.

"Good evening, Mr. Markwick," Thaxton said with a too-exaggerated bow. "Come to the last supper?"

⚜

Thaxton, by that time in the course of the day, just wanted to wrap his hands around Miles's neck and get it over with. He had actually contemplated his chances of getting away with such a thing—temporary insanity. *Oh, yes, I am indeed a viscount from a very old family, your honor, ever so sorry.* He might have gotten away with it, but not somewhere so public as a dinner.

Miles did not answer. He gave him the cut direct, in fact.

Cassandra did not. She held his gaze, had not even glanced at Miles. He had expected her to have some sort of expression, whether it was of horror or something else, but her face set itself in passive lines. Placid ones, even. As if nothing out of the ordinary had occurred in her entire lifetime.

He turned back to his father and the dowager, half listening to their conversation as dinner plates began circulating the room. Their afternoon together had done his father a vast good. He did not seem to remember everything that Spencer's mother was talking about, but instead of throwing a frustrated fit, he had nodded politely. Her patience made Thaxton think of his own behavior when dealing with his father . . . which was decidedly less patient.

The uncomfortable feeling in the pit of his stomach told Thaxton that he might have been doing something wrong. A few things.

Dinner passed in pleasant nonsense, since their table had been loaded with people who knew what tomorrow held or would not ask intrusive questions. Quite smart of the countess. Arabella kept things light, and her husband was surprisingly witty; they ended up being the pair Thaxton listened to for most of the meal. The dowager and his father kept up their chatter, Lady Dorset bent Spencer's ear about country versus city living, and both Eliza and Cassandra drifted in and out of various threads of conversation.

Such as now, when the countess picked up the earl saying that he did not leave the house very much anymore.

"Do you not go outside?" she asked, too politely, as if she were ashamed that she could not hold the question back.

"No, not anymore," the earl answered with no malice. "Jonathan does not think it best."

"That is . . ." Thaxton started, his words snarling on the way from his brain to his mouth. "That is not exactly true. It is for his own safety."

Though Cassandra did not turn, he saw her neck extend, so subtly.

"I did miss parties," the Earl Vane said, his eyes scanning the room in their usual way, not settling on anything in particular.

"We are so glad you came," the dowager said, a smile softening her wrinkled face. As the earl had gotten better in her company, she was less stern for the shared memories, more accepting. Spencer threw Thaxton a look from his seat at the head of the table.

Thaxton pursed his lips and took a long drink of wine before he realized he was doing so. The alcohol hit his palate with a force that took him aback. He wanted more; he needed to obliterate the awkward sensation of owning up to his choices. He held the stem of the glass, weighing his options. This could be his last night on earth.

Better to experience it fully, then. He put the glass down.

Cassandra's mouth turned up in the tiniest smile.

When the dinner ended and the company parted along gender lines, those men involved in the duel were to meet again in Spencer's study. Thaxton was more than surprised when he found his father in the middle of that meeting. He raised his eyebrows, about to demand an explanation, but Spencer spoke first.

"Thaxton, sit," Spencer ordered gravely when he entered. "There is an issue."

Thaxton stood beside a chair but could not force himself to sit. Sutton lurked behind Spencer, presumably awaiting any task.

"Father? Has no one told you this is a private meeting?"

The Earl Vane smiled, as if there was nothing wrong with the situation.

"I am standing on Miles's honor, of course."

Thaxton sputtered. "That. Is that a joke?"

Miles spoke from his seat next to the earl.

"Far from it. Your father is the only man I have found at this god-forsaken house party willing to stand on my honor. The whole affair quite has me wondering what kind of company the Spencers keep, and I shall say so when I get back to town."

"Come off it," Spencer said. "You will do no such thing. You would ruin your invitation list, and you could not bear it."

"You must pick a new second," Thaxton insisted. "You cannot do this."

Miles smirked.

"Can't I? Unless you would like to go on record as saying your father is not well enough to be considered in charge of his faculties, I do not see another choice."

Thaxton's eyes found Spencer's as he stood very still behind his desk. The Earl Vane turned, looking up.

"I am in charge of my faculties, gentlemen," he said.

Thaxton disagreed. "You have to stop this, Percy."

Spencer crossed his arms, his eyes saying so much more than his words subsequently did. "I would have to declare your father unfit."

"I am not unfit," the Earl Vane said, almost sounding like his old self.

Miles leaned back in his chair, satisfied.

"Father," Thaxton said, barely able to keep the humiliating tremolo out of his voice, "you are standing for Miles's honor against your own son. Do you not think that odd?"

"Not at all, my dear boy. Spencer is already standing for your honor; you are taken care of—poor cousin Miles has no one."

Thaxton directed his gaze to poor cousin Miles.

"This is a long way to go to hurt me further. You do realize that the satisfaction of my father standing on your side means that he will be the one handling your gun."

"I am well versed in the handling of dueling pistols," the Earl Vane said, a slight offended cast to his tone.

"No one disputes that, Father."

"I do not think this wise," Spencer said, "but if Miles has asked and the earl has accepted, there is nothing we can do. Short of . . ."

"We are not doing *that*," Thaxton said.

"Spencer and I have many things to discuss," the Earl Vane said. "So, if the duelists will leave the room, we can get started."

There was nothing more to it. Thaxton turned, numb to his core, and left Spencer's study. He did not turn to see if Miles was behind him. He did not turn to see Spencer's sad resolve, an expression he knew well.

He almost did not see Miss Seton when he rounded the corner to his suite.

❦❦❦

After the time she had bided in the shadows by his door, Cassandra did not expect Thaxton to brush by her. At first, he looked focused on getting into his foyer as fast as possible, as if he was fleeing from something. Then he stopped, fingers on the metal, and spoke without so much as glancing at her.

"Cassandra. I was not sure you'd come."

"I wanted to stay away, but I could not."

"Come in," he said, still not turning to look at her.

She slipped in behind him, and he locked the door, his eyes meeting hers at last.

"Have you been trying to ignore me? Deliberately?"

"Yes."

"You are not very good at it."

"I know." She smiled. "You have the advantage. Even though you say you will not die tomorrow, I cannot overlook the possibility. Have a drink with me before you sleep?"

"I came back here to do that, in fact. Miles has chosen his second."

She crossed to the bar, deciding it best to give explicit permission, after all her haranguing about alcohol. However, the more she thought about it, through the painful dinner and the hour with the ladies afterward, she realized that Thaxton must be feeling rather set-upon and alone. She could only rationalize that he deserved that feeling for so long, because she was in love with him.

And love made one do things that ran contrary to logic.

She poured a glass of what she assumed was scotch and handed it to him. He nodded and sat down in a chair next to a fire.

"He chose my father."

"That has to be against the rules," she said, sitting across from him. "Is it some kind of joke?"

He took a sip of his drink. "I am deadly serious."

"But your father . . ."

". . . is not well, yes. But my entire existence has been devoted to that fact not being public knowledge."

"Is there no rule against this sort of thing?"

"There are no proper rules. Just some old Irish pamphlet that molds in most men's pistol boxes."

Cassandra took a drink, using all of her will to appear unaffected by the sting.

"Evidently it is more important to Miles to irritate you than to have a properly loaded pistol when he faces you on the field."

"My thoughts exactly."

Thaxton was silent for a long moment, inhaling the odor of his drink but not ingesting it. He stared at the fire, as Cassandra imagined one would do if one were he, holding the past close with resentment, afraid to move into the future.

"He seems well, though. My father."

"Yes, he handled himself well through dinner." Cassandra reached for the best way to phrase it without being offensive. "I am sure that the rest of the party found no fault with his behavior."

"Yes, but they were watching for it. For anything that might seem amiss. The story of a mad earl is more salacious than that of an aging mind."

"And that is it exactly, Jonathan. It is time that you stopped caring what they think." The drink was working the same wonder it had the other night, loosening her tongue and setting forth the truth of what she felt. "It will not serve us well in the future if you care what people think. They will say worse of me than they ever did your father."

Thaxton set down his glass and leaned forward, taking her hand.

"Cassandra."

She could no longer look into his eyes and wish she felt nothing; she wanted to have this love even though it hurt. If it were a thing she must endure, then she would endure it.

"The beginning of our relationship has not been smooth," he said, "but I promise you that the worst is almost over. I will wed you in Scotland before anyone can lodge a protest."

"But my parents . . ."

". . . wanted to give you to Miles Markwick. They did not exactly have your best interests at heart."

Even as she had been advising him to not care about what people said of his father, she worried ceaselessly what people were going to think of her. It was not as if she could marry Thaxton and go about having the polite society life that she had always envisioned. They would be lucky if the Spencers could invite them to parties without causing gossip. They would never be hosting any house party at the Vane estate.

None of that was enough cost to abandon him.

"Do not get killed," she said, "and we will leave immediately."

"Agreed. Good."

"But for the sake of argument," she said, the tinge of alcohol rusting her voice, "if tonight was your last night on earth, what would you want to be doing?"

"Less talking," he said, taking both of her hands now, kissing them in turn as he pulled her to her feet. "Or at least less talking about unpleasantness."

She smiled up at him, and he wrapped his arms around her waist.

"That sounds perfect," she said, her lips nearing his. He tilted down, meeting her halfway. The kiss turned her smile into another form of communication. She returned his fervor, trying to say all the things she could not find words for.

Before long, his hands, large and restless, began wandering. His fingers skittered up her neck, tracing the path of her collarbone until he found the chain that held his ring. He pulled it out of her bodice, rolling the sapphire in the pads of his fingers.

"I will put this on your hand, proper, before the week is out."

She fought a wave of melancholy—it was a promise he could not make for sure. Neither of them could predict what would happen at dawn, but she did not want to argue. He caught the fleeting look on her face and kissed her again.

"No unpleasantness," he whispered, his tongue tracing out, erasing the taut line.

No more words could make their way past the barrier of the kiss, and she surrendered to it, to feeling instead of thought. She found the buttons on his dinner jacket, working them free one by one.

Her initiative must have pleased him; she could feel a new strain in his trousers. Those buttons followed logically, so she released them, pausing to draw her palm over the growing hardness.

"Cassie," he groaned.

She met his eyes.

"I just want to remind you how good it is to be alive."

"Very effective," he said, sliding the jacket from his shoulders and dropping it on a nearby chair. His undergarments were visible at his waistline as he backed her toward his bed.

Thaxton pushed her lightly and she fell back, skirts billowing into the duvet. She started to reach behind to undo her corset, but his look stopped her.

"No," he said. "Me first."

Just the thought of him naked before her, while she lay fully clothed, felt impossibly decadent. He turned his back to her, working on his boots.

"No footwear in the bedroom of our house. Takes too much time."

He dropped both boots, soft thuds on the carpet, then turned to gently pull off her slippers. Thaxton stood again, extinguishing the two oil lamps on the side of the bed, but leaving the candles lit. He slipped out of his waistcoat, returning to the foot of the bed, slowly getting rid of his trousers. She watched as he pulled down his undergarments, and followed the line of his hipbone, prominent. Cassandra had found another favorite part of Thaxton by his undressing so leisurely. When he was naked, already hard, his eyes went dark in the shadows, his voice low.

"Turn around."

She did as he asked, though it robbed her of the view. He climbed on top of her, an expanse of skin against the fine fabric, setting her on fire. This time when he unlaced her corset, it did not take as long, eager fingers working steadily. She inwardly praised her foresight in not wearing the usual architecture under her dress—there was no barrier between the silk and him. She felt his hand reach between her legs, his thumb covered in the fabric, working against the sensitive nub that turned on her passion. She was starting to think of it as a button, one that switched off her mind. His soft circling made her lift her behind and moan, which he replied to with a husky laugh.

"So beautiful," he said, drawing back to turn her around again. He wrestled with the dress, impatient, kissing the skin he exposed. He gave one last good pull and the dress came off, slipping over her legs, a waterfall of silk to the floor.

Thaxton did not bother taking off her chemise, just hiked it up over her thighs as he covered her body with his. His shaft pressed into her, throbbing, and his hands found her breasts. He pinched her nipples through the chemise, the combination of both sensations making her hips move restlessly.

"Jonathan," she groaned.

"Yes?" He smiled, looking at her while he grasped his base, guiding the tip to her wetness. She rose up, pushing him in farther, watching the smug look disappear from his face. He closed his eyes as she settled around him, stretched for him.

She kept moving her hips, little circles, angling up to feel more of him, deeper.

"Oh," she said, surprising herself. "Oh, my."

"Yes," he said again, hoarsely, his eyes intense and glazed. "Yes, let me see."

Cassandra did not know exactly what he was asking. He did not begin to thrust, and she could not help her own movements, grinding him in deeper still, until he was as sheathed as possible. His hand returned to that place, her center, and she closed her eyes. She was so full of pleasure that it felt like delirium. She felt herself building to that peak again, the one he made her chase, and just as her climax started, he began to thrust.

She spasmed, the unbelievable feeling extending, going on far longer than she thought possible. He moaned, his breath increasing with his speed. The chemise stuck to her skin, and his hands moved under her, cupping her to bring her in closer. Thaxton released a long groan, his whole body tensing, motionless as he spilled inside of her.

He did not move for a moment, and Cassandra relished his weight on top of her, the reality of him, solid. He still jumped inside of her, and she wiggled, kissing his neck.

"I do not want to return to my room," she said with a smile.

"Oh, not yet," he said, nuzzling her back. "I am not yet tired . . . and there are other positions to explore."

A few others, she found out, and even then they had not exhausted his knowledge.

She did not mean to fall asleep in his arms, but she did so anyway.

Cassandra woke in the middle of the night and carefully slid from under the weight of Thaxton's arm. She snuck back to her room and slept for what felt like only a half hour, then woke again. She had a moment of sheer panic, unsure of the time. The ladies were meeting at 5:00 a.m., absolutely no later.

The plain dress she chose had no frills or adornment to get in the way. She paired it with her sturdiest walking boots, anticipating a bit of running. Best to be prepared.

None of the servants stirred yet, but it was all the same to her. Cassandra did not want to eat, nor did she want to try to explain her early rise. The estate held the quiet of a massing storm cloud, right before it opened up. There was a soft knock at her door.

"Come in," she whispered.

Eliza opened the door enough to slip through. "Percy is asleep. I have no idea why he is so calm . . . he slept like an innocent last night. He did keep asking me if I was cross, which I was, but he eventually let it drop."

"I saw Jonathan; I could not help it."

Eliza smiled. "I knew you would. Is he well?"

"He is very upset by his father. He is startlingly unmoved, however, by the specter of possible death."

"That—I cannot believe I am about to say this—that is normal. For him."

"Do you think we will be able to stop them?"

The countess took a moment before answering, which spoke volumes. Cassandra had always known Eliza to be decisive. If there was a problem, she knew her mind and she made a decision, a skill Cassandra had always envied. But the answer to this particular issue had not emerged overnight.

"I do not know. But we have to try."

There was another soft knock, and Lucy opened the door without being told. The women's eyes passed over each other, quickly assessing. Lucy's eyes had a determined set to them, her posture rigid. More like the woman who had first walked into the séance, less like the woman of the past few days, practically broken.

"Are we ready?" she asked.

Cassandra came forward, taking her hand.

"Are *you* ready? That is the most important part. This all hinges on you."

"I am," Lucy said, her voice filled with resolve. "He deserves it."

"Thank you," Cassandra said earnestly, letting go of her hand. "Thank you so much for doing this."

"It is the least I owe you, after what I put you through."

"Not you. Miles."

"I should not have been so blind for so long."

"It is the past," Eliza said. "We need to focus on now. Lucy, you are to be posted in the copse of trees on the left of the dueling field, behind Miles, but out of Thaxton's firing line. We are hoping to interrupt before anyone can shoot. Cassie and I will be posted on the right, nearest to Thaxton. We will wait until we hear you begin."

"I do not know how he will react," Lucy said, her eyes far off for a moment. "If he gets angry, I cannot predict what he might do."

"I could say the same of Thaxton," Cassandra mused. She straightened her back. "Ladies. Places."

Chapter Eleven

Thaxton had been up for hours. He strolled through the mist floating from the edges of the pond, making it to the dueling field first. After loving Cassandra the best way he could, he felt that her passing out from pleasure was the highest compliment. And he felt he had never done anything more important in his life.

If he were to die, he was as ready as he could be.

"You are early," Spencer said, his voice a little strained, having briskly hiked the two hills that separated the pond and its surroundings from the rest of the estate. He had the box of dueling pistols tucked under his arm.

"Fitful sleep. It never much mattered to me, anyway."

"You've been cataloging things that matter?"

"Ceaselessly. There are a lot of things I had not thought about."

"Funny how a woman will make you do that."

"They are right, you know."

"Of course they are," Spencer said, his hair half covering his face in the sudden wind over the landscape. "But we cannot change our wrongness. It is tradition."

"It is asinine."

Spencer shrugged, an adolescent gesture that looked strange on shoulders weighed down by an earldom.

"It is, but what is done is done. How many shots do you think it will take to sufficiently scare Miles?"

"I was just going to make him bleed horribly, until he chose my father as his second. Now I may actually kill him."

Thaxton paced ten away from the middle of the field, eyeing the copse of trees that marked the edges of the dueling ground. He paced ten back to Spencer. He must have completed that movement fifteen times that morning, this iteration making for sixteen.

"Let's not," Spencer said. "Messy. I do not want to explain a death at my very first house party. It is bad enough that it will most likely be remembered as the weekend Dorset's daughter ran off with the mad viscount."

Thaxton smiled despite himself. "Likely."

"One more thing, before Miles and your father arrive. I would like to propose your father stay on here, while you enjoy your shameful honeymoon."

"Spence, no, what a hideous imposition . . ."

"Not at all. Talking with my mother is not only doing him much good but also making her happy. You would be doing me a favor. She has little to occupy her in the dower house."

"I could not—"

"Just say thank you, Jonathan. I assure you, it is easier than you make it seem."

"Thank you." He smiled.

Spencer placed the box of pistols on a high table that had been positioned for that purpose, probably in the even earlier hours by Sutton. Even now, the butler lurked near Spencer, in the case that the earl might have a command. The many days that had passed had done nothing to endear the valet to him—his constant watchfulness unnerved Thaxton.

Miles crested the hill, followed at some distance by the Earl Vane. Thaxton frowned, holding back a growl. Miles was not even good enough to stay behind when the earl was struggling. He wanted to call out, but discretion was the order of the morning, so he settled for curling and uncurling his fist.

When they were within earshot, he did not hold back, his voice a low hiss.

"Good of you to make sure my father is taken care of, Markwick."

Over the years, Thaxton had noticed that Miles had a special smile he reserved for when he was pleased with his cruelty.

"The Earl Vane has assured me that he needs no special treatment."

Spencer came forward, taking the earl's arm and guiding him over to the small table.

"We will begin checking the pistols," he said in a low, no-nonsense tone.

Thaxton glared at Miles. They had somehow set themselves in the middle of the field already, facing each other. Miles, a little shorter, took the opportunity to turn up his nose.

"If you survive this," he sneered, "I rather think you should retire to the country. No one will want to see you in London again."

"You seem to be under the impression that people care about your opinion, Markwick, yet you could only come up with a confused old man to stand on your honor. And you say I am delusional."

"You are a laughingstock."

The click of a barrel sounded behind them, and Thaxton turned to see his father, cocking the pistol that Miles would soon be raising.

"Then it will look all the worse when you have to cede," Thaxton murmured. Somehow, in the midst of everything, the dreamlike crawl of fog on the ground and the evil quiet, an assuredness had stolen over him.

It would all be over soon, and he would still be standing.

He was not doomed, nor had he ever been.

"We are ready to begin," Spencer said. "The seconds agree on the integrity of the weapons. They also agree that no peaceful solution could be met between the duelists."

"May we have the pistols?" Thaxton asked.

Spencer came up beside him, carefully handing over the percussion-barrel masterpiece. The rich wood of the handle, the polished engravings on the metal, lions roaring in etched lines. Thaxton turned it over in his hands, looking at his family crest. There, tiny and deeply engraved, was that same symbol that had been drawn so gruesomely in blood on his door.

His father handed the other pistol to Miles.

Thaxton looked up, into Miles's fathomless, animal eyes, and put one arm behind his back. The other held the pistol at his side, his thumb finding purchase on the back on the hammer. Miles followed suit, tense and straight. Thaxton took a moment for triumph, turning his left wrist so that his cuff link glinted. He wore the very pair of cuff links that Cassandra had taken out of Lucy's drawer, diamond-shaped and engraved with *MRM*.

Thaxton saw recognition in Miles's eyes, right before they turned.

"On my count, gentlemen. Turn and walk ten paces."

Spencer's oratory training hid any emotion from the pronouncement. Miles and Thaxton turned, but not before the latter managed one more hurried glare.

"One," Spencer said.

Thaxton took the step forward, hearing Miles's boots crunch on the grass.

"Two."

The pond stretched out on his left, the water placid and shimmering.

"Three."

His stride was unchanged. It seemed he could feel Miles behind him.

"Four."

There was a wail.

Not any wail. The same wail that had brought him down to the blue parlor the night he and Cassandra first kissed. Lengthy, grief-stricken, keening. Coming from . . . behind him?

"Stop," he ordered. "Stop."

Spencer raised a hand. "What is it, Thaxton?"

The wail sounded again, at once close and far away. A distinctive noise, it was the very same one from that fateful night, a banshee expressing her extreme heartache.

"Do you not hear that?"

Thaxton turned back around, seeing that Miles already had.

"Pistols on the ground," he said and lowered his own slowly, watching that Miles did the same. They both crouched, looking at each other. Thaxton let go of his gun first and drew back up to his feet. The wail came again, unmistakable this time, near.

"I heard it," the Earl Vane said.

"As did I," Spencer confirmed.

"I hear nothing," Miles said with a slight tremor.

As if on cue to prove him wrong, it came again.

"I think it is coming from the trees behind Markwick," Spencer said as the wail tapered off.

Miles looked over his shoulder. "Could not be. I am sure I hear nothing."

Again. Inimitable. Loud.

Thaxton could no longer wait. He tramped forward, peering between the trees. He did not have to go far into the copse before he saw a flash of blonde hair.

"Lucy Macallister," he said, loud enough for the other men to hear. Spencer was not far behind him, followed by the Earl Vane. Miles had not moved.

"Lord Thaxton."

She turned, her head held high.

"You are the wailing woman."

"Ever have been." Lucy watched as Miles regained the use of his limbs and joined them. His eyes were on hers, as if the dueling field had disappeared.

"What are you doing here?" he said.

Her posture remained the same: proud.

"Making amends."

❧❦❧

"Now," Cassandra said.

She and Eliza crept out onto the field while the men's backs were turned. They each bent down, carefully scooping up the dueling pistols and inching back behind the cover of trees.

"They did not see us," Eliza whispered. "We did it."

"Shh, we can almost hear what they are saying."

Lucy's voice, nearer than the others, floated toward them.

"Miles has been plotting against Thaxton all this time. He knew you were onto him but felt assured you did not have any proof. I am ready to be that proof."

". . . picked a more proper time . . ." Cassandra heard Spencer say. Eliza rolled her eyes.

"There was no other time, my lord. I have been a coward until now. My instinct was to hide my head in shame, after what Miles has done. What he convinced me to go along with."

"And what was that?" Thaxton's voice was loud, clear as a bell and furious.

"The séances, as you know, were faked. But even before that, Miles snuck me in by bribing a groom to act as the wailing woman. There is a vent in the blue parlor that goes to your room; that was the first step. He thought you would question your sanity, but he did not plan on Cassandra hearing as well. Miles planned to have you declared unfit,

Lord Thaxton, mad, by burden of proof. He has a paper signed by your father, saying the estate is entrusted to him if you are not fit to run it."

There was absolute silence.

"Father?" Thaxton said finally. "Is this true?"

"Do you not think it best? I meant to speak with you about it." The earl's voice held certainty, as if he could not conceive that he had done anything wrong. Cassandra realized she and Eliza had inched over, behind Lucy yet still in the woods, so that they could hear nearly every word now.

"Miles was concerned about the estate," the earl continued. "I assumed you would be pleased with my forethought. You are always so worried about running things and . . . you have not seemed well."

The disbelief was evident in Thaxton's voice.

"*I* have not been well? *I*, father?"

"You do not talk to me. You drink incessantly. You are cross all the time."

"So you thought to give the estate to *my third cousin*?"

"Not give it to him, exactly. Only in the case that we were both unfit."

Miles, who had been standing stock-still, finally said something.

"It would have been entirely appropriate. I am ready to take up an estate, in need of the funds, and engaged to be married. In a perfect position. Thaxton, on the other hand, has been reeling around Spencer House for two weeks, painting with blood and communicating with spirits."

"You know that is not the truth," Lucy said.

"I am finished," Thaxton growled, stalking back to the field. Cassandra moved through the trees, following him as best she could, trying not to snap any branches. Thaxton reached his former spot and knelt down, searching through the grass.

"I am finished dealing with you in any other way than at the end of a barrel. Where . . . the bloody hell . . . is my pistol?"

Cassandra looked down at the gun in her hand and smiled.

"They are both gone," she heard Miles say. "Both guns are gone."

The men retook the clearing, and Cassandra could see both Miles and Thaxton. She stayed behind the tree nearest to the field of play, the gun at her side. She shook it and the bullet inside fell to the grass. Spencer's frame came into her view, crouching on the ground, his hands carefully searching.

"Where are the damned pistols?" he muttered, barely audible.

Eliza snickered, looking at Cassandra and turning over the one she was holding, releasing the other bullet. She nodded, and Cassandra stepped onto the field, Thaxton's pistol raised and leveled at Miles.

"Good morning," she said brightly.

He stopped where he was, straightening his back to regard her.

"Cassandra." He put his hands out, palms up, and took a step toward her. "Let's put that down."

Eliza, behind her, raised the other pistol.

"Let us not move any farther, Mr. Markwick."

Cassandra smiled.

Miles lifted his hands in the air, removing the foot he had put forward. No one else moved.

"Who are these women?" the Earl Vane asked. He squinted, making Cassandra worry about the fact that he had been cleared to be a second, which required sight.

She kept her eyes on Miles, feeling Eliza's pistol over her shoulder.

"My lord, hello. We met. Cassandra Seton. I am engaged to your son and dreadfully sorry you are finding out at this moment."

"Oh!" the Earl Vane exclaimed, clapping his hands together. "The girl."

"Apologies," Eliza added. "I did not intend for a duel to be house-party entertainment."

"This is all very exciting," he said offhandedly, as if he were watching a play.

"If you will excuse us," Cassandra said to him kindly, "there is a matter that must be immediately dealt with concerning your cousin."

The earl nodded, stately. "Of course."

She raised the pistol a little higher, aiming the empty barrel at Miles's heart.

"You have no idea how to use that," he said, sounding unsure.

She cocked the hammer.

"Oh? Do I not?"

She did not, not really, but she was sure she could make a show of it. She could see Thaxton peripherally, but enough to know that he was smiling.

"What can I do for you, Miss Seton?" Miles asked, his hands in a defensive posture.

"First of all, you will relinquish your previous claim on my hand. If you do so, Lucy Macallister and I will not go to the constable with the story about what you tried to do to the poor viscount."

Miles eyes were drawn to Lucy at her name.

"I told her everything, have no doubt," Lucy said, taking up the thread of conversation. "Secondly, you will leave England without a word to anyone about what has transpired here. Go back to your pathetic estate and molder there. I am staying on with the London Spiritualist Society, and I have no wish to ever see your face again."

"We are through?"

"You are, at least," Lucy scoffed, her words colored with disbelief.

Thaxton spoke finally.

"I must say—if I may interject—this is quite brilliant."

"Thank you," Lucy and Cassandra said at the same time.

"If I agree, what?" Miles said. "I am free to go?"

"In a sense," Cassandra said. "You will have to live with yourself, and none of us envy you that."

"Too right," Thaxton said.

He sounded a little too smug, Cassandra thought. She swiveled the gun at him. He did not flinch.

"And you," she said.

"Anything, my love."

"You and I are leaving in an hour to go directly to a chapel."

"I had hoped."

"But when we return, we will not be living as hermits or running away from society. We are not going to hide your father away like an invalid. We will be facing our issues head-on and not drinking them away."

"I suppose I can manage that," he said, "if you would put the gun down."

Eliza, gun still trained on Miles, spoke.

"We are all in agreement? Spencer, you will supervise Miles's letter to the Marquess of Dorset that he is bowing out of the engagement, while Thaxton and Cassie speak to Lady Dorset. Then, Mr. Markwick, I will have you off my premises immediately. All that talk of Thaxton being mad, when you were the one running around killing ravens."

Miles took one glance at Lucy, a last plea.

"You could come with me. We can forget about the past. I will forgive you for what you have done today."

"Not if you were the last man on earth," she said.

"Come along, Markwick," Spencer said. Though he had been silent, he glanced at Eliza with the gun, a tiny, proud smile on his face. "Feel free to lower the pistols anytime, ladies."

Neither woman did so until Spencer and Markwick had crested the hill back to the estate. Thaxton opened the dueling box and offered it to them in turn, so they placed the pistols carefully back in.

"I knew they were not loaded," he said, "but that does not change the fact that you ladies saved the day."

"Somebody had to do so." Cassandra smiled. "You certainly were not up for the job."

He came over to her and took her in his arms.

"Thank you," he whispered, right before kissing her, in full view of everyone.

"Good show, son," the Earl Vane said.

"Much to be done now," Eliza said with a smile. "But first . . . break-fast. Come now, Earl Vane, let me escort you back to the house. I am sure Thaxton and Miss Seton have some things they need to discuss."

Thaxton had not let go of her and seemed to be making no move in that direction.

"We will be right along." He smiled at the countess.

"I am sorry I had to point a gun at you," Cassandra said when they had gone, looking up at Thaxton. His lips were in a markedly amused line. "But you would not listen to reason."

"You are forgiven. And truthfully, it was a rather alluring picture."

She hit him on the arm. "Oh, enough. It should not have come to this. And I was very wrong about Lucy's motives."

"I was wrong about my father," he said. "I was wrong about the curse. Oh god, darling, I have done so many things wrong. I was wrong to not listen to y—"

Cassandra put her fingers on his lips.

"Stop." She smiled slyly. "I am sick to death of your mawkish soliloquies."

"You will have to distract me." He grinned, tickling her sides. He pulled her into another kiss, one that went on far too long for them to be in the middle of an open field while it continued. He pulled back, his eyes shining. "I am sure we can find privacy . . . even a bed. Do not let me get maudlin."

"I am beginning to think you use that as an excuse," she said with a suspicious raise of her eyebrow.

"Maybe so," he said, pulling her toward the house. "Maybe so."

තⓔන

Outside the parlor, Thaxton held on to Cassandra's hand. By early after-noon, they could no longer ignore the necessity of telling Lady Dorset about the change in arrangements. Not the duel, though. They need not go wild with the confessions.

"We have to go in," he said. She had been stalling.

"I know," Cassandra replied. She still did not move.

The door opened, Lady Dorset's hand on the knob. It was rare that she would open a door herself, and she wore a mighty scowl. Thaxton countered it with a big smile. As mothers-in-law went, he could handle her. All bluster.

"I can hear you two," Lady Dorset snapped. "So you may as well come in."

"Thank you," Thaxton said, walking into the brightly lit receiving parlor. The overall cheerful impression of the room, dotted with yellow accents in pillows and drapes, directly contradicted the angry woman standing in the center of it. Cassandra hid behind him, quite odd considering that a few hours ago she had been pointing a gun, fearless.

"Miles has already been to see me, so I approve of the guilty looks on your faces. You should be ashamed of yourselves."

Thaxton felt Cassandra bristle, as if she wanted to say something. He reached back for her hand to give it a reassuring squeeze.

"We understand this must be awkward, my lady," Thaxton said. Even though the woman thought he was mad, he remained her social superior. He hoped it was enough to stop a full-blown argument. "However, as I am sure Miles has told you, I will be marrying Miss Seton."

"*Lady* Cassandra."

"Miss Seton. Until she is Viscountess Thaxton, then Countess Vane. You would do well to remember."

"Well," Lady Dorset said, her tone making it clear she could find no other words.

"We will be leaving this evening," he continued, not waiting for her to respond further. "I have already written to Lord Dorset. Respectfully, of course."

"Of course," she echoed.

"If Lord Dorset will allow it, Cassandra and I will visit in two months after our wedding date. I trust by then you will have decided it is easy to be civil."

Lady Dorset's mouth was open a little. Thaxton smiled, glancing back at Cassandra. She looked as he expected—a bit shocked, a lot pleased. His strategy of just barreling over her stepmother had worked better than he hoped.

"Now, if you do not mind, we should prepare to travel." Thaxton bowed his head. "Good afternoon, my lady."

He started to leave, assuming Cassandra would follow. She did not. He turned back to see her eyes locked with Lady Dorset's. He could only imagine what Cassandra was thinking, now free of the woman who had run her life for so long. There was not fear on her face anymore. Thaxton watched her chin lift just a fraction, her mouth slant in a satisfied smile.

"Cassie," he said softly.

Her attention snapped back, and she smiled over at him. She inclined her head to her stepmother—not a gesture of respect, merely farewell—then fairly skipped out of the room with him.

Epilogue

Four Months Later

Thaxton ran up the stairs of Vane Manor, two at a time, breathless by the time he got to the top.

"Darling?" he called.

Cassandra's voice rang out from the parlor.

"Back here, darling. With Lucy."

Thaxton poked his head around the corner, finding his wife bent over a table with Lucy Macallister, peering at papers.

"Have you seen Papa?" he said.

Cassandra looked up, smiling. He wondered if it would ever cease to tug his heart when she smiled at him. He thought not.

"He is in the garden," she said. "The chaplain stopped by unannounced, and they are having tea in the garden."

Thaxton smiled over at Lucy. "Sorry to interrupt."

"No, no, it is fine," Lucy said, smiling back. "We were just going over plans for the workshop that Eliza wants to have next week."

"You have been busy," Thaxton said. "All the work with the London Spiritualist Society seems to be going quite well."

"It is even better than I imagined," Lucy said, a wistful note in her voice.

Cassandra wiggled her eyebrows. "There is a man," she sang.

"Oh, Miss Macallister." Thaxton grinned. "How very scandalous."

"You two should talk," Lucy said, her eyes back down to the papers. "Even if it becomes something, it will never be the spectacle that you caused."

It had been quite too much for the first month or so. They had a stream of visitors once they returned from their honeymoon, both well-meaning people and gossipmongers. Cassandra handled it all with aplomb; she and Eliza frequently joked that their headmistress had prepared them almost too well for this sort of task.

The month after that, they were able to stay quiet. They settled into the old manor that was rarely used, so close to Spencer House. They all needed it, most of all Thaxton's father. It helped the earl immensely to be in the home he grew up in, near his oldest remaining friends who all understood his condition.

Four months earlier, Thaxton would have thought it a fantasy.

"I should get back to London," Lucy said. "I have so much work to do. I only meant to stay two days, but Cassandra's hospitality is addictive."

"You should just pack a larger trunk every time you come, Lucy. I do not like you traveling all this way for short stays."

"It does seem silly," Thaxton said.

"Perhaps next time I can bring . . . Edward."

"Of course." Cassandra smiled.

Thaxton crossed over to her, wrapping an arm around her waist. They never felt they had to hide their affection from Lucy; she had become, in a strange way, like family. The beginning of their friendship had been fraught, to understate the situation. Thaxton was glad that was not public knowledge, the terrible folly of Markwick and his manipulation. If Lucy had been forced to repeat the humiliation of his betrayal, it would have broken her. Instead, she was steadily building a good life for herself, surrounded by people who cared about her.

In effect, Miles Markwick had given them all gifts.

Society at large just thought Thaxton had stolen his fiancée and run him off. It had actually improved his reputation. Made him into something of a lothario, a distant and mysterious man reformed by love. He did not hate it, being seen so.

And it was not entirely untrue, really.

"Oh, I meant to tell you both," Lucy said. "Miles is back in Scotland. He tried to petition my father for my hand, thinking that I had not written them about his duplicity. Naive of him, don't you think?"

"He is not the smartest man," Cassandra said, cuddling farther into Thaxton's side.

"No, he did not prove to be. But I am better off for the experience, I can finally say that." Lucy smiled. "And now I will cherish the image of my father forcibly lifting him and throwing him out of the house."

Thaxton smirked to himself, imagining the same thing. It was a madly gratifying image. Evidently, they were all taking a moment to think of it with the silence.

"We probably should not be doing this with such glee," Cassandra remarked.

"Oh, I think I have earned the right," Thaxton said.

Lucy shook herself out of her reverie and leaned forward, kissing Cassandra on the cheek.

"I shall pack," she said. "Thank you, as always. Tell Eliza I will see her soon."

Thaxton watched Lucy swirl out of the room, smiling at the way she had started wearing gauzy gray and purple dresses. It made her look slightly spooky and likely heightened her séance attendees' experience. She had left behind Miles and started to build an image, a reputation all her own.

"She seems to be recovering nicely," he said.

"I could not have hoped for more." Cassandra turned so that she was facing him, wrapping her arms around his waist. "I admit I was worried about her, and I just felt so awful, being so utterly besotted, after what happened with her and Miles."

He pulled her into him tighter.

"Utterly besotted, hmm?"

"Embarrassingly so." She tilted her head up, her lips hovering near his, but not touching just yet. "With a madman. You may have heard."

"Ah, yes," he said, running a hand down her cheek. "The Ghost. I heard that he stole you away from some no-account minor landholder."

"Oh? I heard that the no-account landholder had left me, and that my father made a deal with you to save my reputation."

"Come now."

"Truly. I heard that while I was shopping today, from a group of women right behind me. They must think me stone-deaf as well. Funny that the family has made no move to defend Miles, and it was so easy for him to just disappear again."

He kissed her forehead, deflecting further mention of the subject of Miles.

"So." He smiled. "Are any of the rumors about us true?"

"Oh, yes. The ones that whisper about how dashing you are now that you are happy are true. The ones that say we are madly in love are right."

"Are there any that say we sneak away in the afternoons?"

"Not yet."

Thaxton grinned, backing Cassandra out of the room, his face near hers.

"Best get started on that one."

A Historical Note on Spiritualism

I don't want you to think that Spiritualism was a fraud. I don't want you to think it was true either, this system of belief that involved communicating with the dead. Our latter-day mediums (like John Edward) are not like the mediums of the Victorian age. That is, the Victorians were not frauds interested in money. They were Christians and non-Christians alike who added the belief of the spirit world into their religious practice. Most mediumship was practiced in a domestic environment, with the women of the household acting as conduits to messages from beyond. Public mediums, such as our Lucy Macallister, were rare and somewhat looked down upon.

The majority of mediums were women seizing power in a world where they had access to none. A lot of them were social crusaders who thought outside of society's stringent standards, and thus were more apt to be engaged in subversive activities. Like sitting people down at a table and attempting to see if they could contact spirits. Their interest did not stop at the paranormal, though. A great number of Spiritualists were also attracted to or involved in what we would now call radical politics. They were advocates for abolition and women's rights; they wrote on both of these subjects in much the same way that they wrote about their religion.

Certainly, we know that many aspects of séances were faked, and others cannot ever be explained away or validated for sure, despite the utmost skepticism. It was the magician Harry Houdini who discovered actual fraud, and I used two pieces of evidence he uncovered in his campaign to expose mediums: the leg straps and the bell rung by foot. Houdini may have wanted to reveal the unscientific methods used in séances, but there is anecdotal evidence that he also respected Margery, the medium he famously exposed.

That fact demonstrates the duality and cognitive dissonance engaged in by both the public and the Spiritualists. Like Fox Mulder, most wanted to believe. Believing did not just serve as a sacred comfort, but as a template in which to work out society's issues without having to answer them directly. Some notable mediums were actresses in the past; others had aspirations. Séances were often personal theater, devised by feminine minds, and used to work out family issues both past and present, and to give advice or guidance. It was a way to influence events and make opinions known without being exactly visible.

Quite brilliant, even if some of it was being done unconsciously. Surely some of the home mediums were not aware of the way they subtly affected family decisions, or they didn't have the language to express their intentions. That means that others must have been conscious of what they were doing. Much the same applied to public mediums—there were those who never admitted to trickery in séances, and some who came clean later on in their lives. Interestingly, no matter the medium, most maintained that Spiritualism was a healthy way to deal with the unknown and a valid religious choice.

The historical equivalent of Lucy's fancy London Spiritualist Society was the British National Association of Spiritualists (BNAS), founded in 1873. There were dozens of these kinds of groups, little copses of Spiritualists who just *had* to be the hippest people of their age. The prospectus of the BNAS actually mentions the group's dedication to wealth redistribution and to remedying the "crying social evils" that result from financial inequality. There were male mediums as well. You'll meet one in the sequel to *The Thirteenth Earl*, which I am writing as we speak.

Women in Spiritualism is too fascinating a subject to be covered in one little historical note, but if it's something that interests you, Alex Owen's book *The Darkened Room* is a very good place to start.

About the Author

Photo © 2014 David Cooper

Evelyn Pryce has written comic books, fronted rock bands, and founded a literacy charity group. Her first novel, *A Man Above Reproach*, won the 2013 Amazon Breakthrough Novel in Romance. Pryce lives in Pittsburgh, Pennsylvania, with three gentlemen—her husband and two cats.